Anonymous

Links with the Absent

Or, Chapters on Correspondence

Anonymous

Links with the Absent
Or, Chapters on Correspondence

ISBN/EAN: 9783337303013

Printed in Europe, USA, Canada, Australia, Japan

Cover: Foto ©Andreas Hilbeck / pixelio.de

More available books at **www.hansebooks.com**

LINKS WITH THE ABSENT;

OR,

Chapters on Correspondence.

BY

A MEMBER OF THE URSULINE COMMUNITY, THURLES.

TRANSLATOR OF 'SOLID VIRTUE,' 'A DEVOUT METHOD OF HEARING MASS, ETC.

R. WASHBOURNE,
18 PATERNOSTER ROW, LONDON.
1882.

TO

THE MOST REVEREND DR. MURRAY,

LORD BISHOP OF MAITLAND,

WHOSE WRITTEN NO LESS THAN HIS SPOKEN WORDS HAVE

SO OFTEN AND SO ABLY ADVOCATED THE CAUSE OF

RELIGION AND EDUCATION,

This little Work is Inscribed,

AS A WEAK TESTIMONY OF DEEPEST VENERATION,

GRATITUDE, AND FILIAL DEVOTEDNESS,

BY

THE AUTHOR.

PREFATORY REMARKS.

THESE pages, the thought of which has been suggested by the absence of anything in the shape of a practical treatise on letter-writing, are now presented to a class of readers at once the most interesting, and, we venture to say, the least critical.

The young people for whom they are principally intended have all our sympathy : what wonder, then, that 'Links with the Absent' has been in very deed a 'labour of love'?

In compiling this little work, care has been taken to give it such a form as to place it within the reach of the least developed intellect, while to even the more mature it may not be devoid of profit. The treatise is divided into two parts—the first embracing the subjects, style, and ceremonial of letters ; the second comprising a summary of the various classes of letters, together with the rules for each class.

The Appendix furnishes specimens of letters;

but it is to be remembered they are given merely
to illustrate the theory set forth in the body of this
little work, and not by any means to be appropriated,
as some of our young friends may be tempted to
think.   Far be it from us to contribute even
remotely to foster a spirit of selfishness; for to
shrink from the trouble of exercising the faculty of
thought for the gratification of those one loves is,
to our mind, not the least reprehensible form of it.

In conclusion, let us hope our little volume will
not entirely fail to fulfil its aim, but that at its
suggestion the sacred ties of kinship will grow more
sacred still, those of friendship more enduring, and
that athwart the seas dividing the loved from the
loving, affection's message may be borne to hearts
hungering for tidings of missed ones at the bidding
of 'Links with the Absent.'

CONTENTS.

LINKS WITH THE ABSENT;

OR,

CHAPTERS ON CORRESPONDENCE.

PRELIMINARY CHAPTER.

The End, Utility and Division of this Treatise.

THE end of the art of letter-writing is to enable the absent to converse with one another.

This being the case, a letter should possess all the qualities of conversation.

Now, conversation should be simple, natural and easy; familiar and courteous with friends; polite with strangers and inferiors; respectful with superiors.

However, it must not be supposed that the ease requisite in a letter excludes all care. This is by no means the case. On the contrary, even in our letters to our most intimate friends we should pay some attention both to the subject and the style. This we owe to our friends and to ourselves.

1

'A letter,' to quote the words of a clever author, 'should be like a visit—bright, inspiriting, a reflex of our best mood. Above all, it should be kind and sympathetic.

'There are letters whose arrival we hail as we should that of a new book by a delightful writer, or the visit of a brilliant acquaintance.

'Again, there are others, the delivery of which, anticipating all the dulness and verbosity with which they are sure to abound, we dread like the incursion of a well-known bore.

'In writing, as in speaking, egotism is a capital offence. We have no more right to be egotistic on paper than we have to be dull and disagreeable.

'We should avoid writing too frequently, or at too great length, of our own losses and misfortunes.'

We are entitled to sympathy from our friends, but we should not make our letters inflictions.

The Utility of the Art of Letter-Writing.

No logic is needed to prove, not merely the utility, but in many instances the absolute necessity of this art.

In every station of life, and at every age, it is requisite to be able to write a letter. There is no one whose social position, worldly interests or friendly intercourse does not oblige him to write a letter. Who is there that has not a request to make, of which self-love or diffidence will prevent the verbal expression ? It may be a pardon one desires to obtain, or mayhap a favour. A letter pleads our cause irresistibly, appeases resentment, touches the heart, and wins for us all that we want.

Which of us has not some one beyond the reach of our voice, whom we long to console, to strengthen, to advise ? It may be a brother in a far-off land. Well, a letter will follow him everywhere, will whisper to his heart such soul-stirring words as will retain him on the path of duty, raise his drooping spirits, it may be lead him back to God.

Again, who has not yearned for news of parents and friends, from whom circumstances have necessitated a separation ? A letter arrives weekly, sometimes daily, telling us of their pleasures, their hopes, their trials, their unabated affection, and thus beguiles the weariness of absence from those at home :

With what mingled emotions of joy and pleasure is it not our wont to welcome the well-known writing of an absent friend !

> " Let others give us gems and gold ;
>   With gems and gold we'd lightly part—
> We take them, but we do not hold,
>   The treasures sacred in the heart.
> Such costly boon may have the power
>   To win our thanks and wake our pride ;
> But dearer is the withered flower
>   That has been worn and thrown aside
>   By those we love.'

Yes! even a withered flower once touched by a

hand we love is precious to us.   What then must be
a letter, whose sentiments that hand has traced,
that heart suggested !

And here a question arises: *Is not everyone who
is capable of writing and thinking, competent to
write a letter ? What need, therefore, is there for a
treatise on the subject ?*

To this we answer, that everyone who can write
and think is without doubt able to write a letter,
or, in other words, is capable of expressing his
thoughts in writing.

But in *the manner* of expressing the thought, is
there not an indefinable something which renders it
more persuasive if it is a favour we ask, *more sub-
missive* if a pardon, *more original* and *sparkling*
when we would call up a smile on some loved face,
more tender if it is affection or gratitude we would
evince ?

All these niceties are not to be learned.   They
are the outcome of taste highly cultivated. Nothing
so effectually accomplishes this as the *careful* reading of *good authors.*

FIRST PART.

FUNDAMENTAL RULES FOR THE ART OF LETTER-WRITING.

THESE will be given in the three following chap ters, and will include :

1. RULES FOR THE SUBJECTS OF LETTERS.
2. RULES FOR THE STYLE OF LETTERS.
3. RULES FOR THE CEREMONIAL OF LETTERS.

CHAPTER I.

RULES FOR THE SUBJECTS OF LETTERS.

BY the subjects of a letter is meant *the matter* of which it is composed. The value of a letter, as of every literary work, is estimated by the thoughts which it embodies, just as that of a purse is estimated by the gold it contains.

By *style* is meant the manner in which these thoughts are expressed. If the style adds nothing to the intrinsic worth of the thought, at least it much enhances the pleasure felt in its perception, and in this way the same idea more easily attains its object of reaching and touching the heart. True, the wine presented in an elegant vessel is not the more delicious because of that, but it gains considerably by being thus set off.

FIRST RULE.

WE SHOULD HAVE SOMETHING TO SAY.

This rule is so plainly dictated by common sense that it seems almost absurd to allude to it here. Still it is not useless to do so, particularly where there is question of a correspondence.

When we write without having any other object in view but personal gratification, we may amuse ourselves by jotting down disconnectedly every idea that suggests itself, but when we are writing to another this is no longer allowable.

We should respect the person, and above all the time, of our correspondent too much to trespass on either unnecessarily.

When writing, therefore, we should always have *some business* to treat of, *some news* to tell, *some feeling* to disclose, *a question* to ask, or *a pleasure* to confer. Such are the topics that should, as a rule, form the substance of every letter. Of course there are exceptions, as, for instance, when we take up our pen merely to have a chat with a friend. But of this we shall speak later on.

Letters for which it is Difficult to find Subjects.

Under this head may be classed those which are imposed by social position or by the exigencies of politeness.

For instance, there are such and such persons to whom we ought to write, yet for whom we have so little affection that even our mind remains a blank in their regard.

Few things are more irksome than the writing of letters of this kind ; but in the Second Part will be found some general ideas that may be useful in such cases. These will not, it is true, enable us to write a valuable letter, but at least they will help us to write a befitting one.

But what in reality can be said in a letter?

Why, everything. Nothing is more accommodating than a letter.

The following is the advice given by Joseph de Maistre to his daughter, who, while yet very young, sometimes complained of having nothing to say : ' You must let your pen run on, my dear child, and tell me everything that comes into your head. You have always four subjects to treat of : *Your joys, your sorrows, your occupations, your longings.* With these one can easily fill up four pages. As for me, I can carry out these four divisions in almost as many words. *My pleasure* would be to be with you ; *my regret* is to be separated from you ; *my occupation* is to discover the' means of going back to you ; *my wish* to succeed in this.'

To this charming piece of advice we would add two others. They refer to our relations with our family and friends.

1st. *Let us open our hearts* to reveal those treasures of affection and friendship, those sentiments of gratitude and esteem which the Almighty has so lavishly given us.

We should never say, when thinking of a friend who expects a letter from us, '*I know not what to say.*'

Have we not *some pleasures* to tell of, *some sorrows* to share, *some amusements* to describe, *some consolation* to impart, *some advice* to ask, *some reminiscences* to recall ? When one feels impelled to write, is it not that the heart, full to overflowing, seeks to vent itself in words ?

A letter that is a disagreeable duty, is rarely a well-written one.

2nd. *We should open our minds.* Truly has the poet sung :

> ' Oh, there are thoughts
> That slumber in the soul, like sweetest sounds.'

But when, if not in writing to a friend, should the dormant thought awake, bringing with it, as it ever must, myriad memories of the past—now bright and joyous, now sad and touching. And written under these impulses, how can our letter fail of giving pleasure ? How many refined and delicate thoughts, lively and ingenious sallies, sparkling and graceful similes, pleasing allusions, grave or playful recitals, quotations, proverbs, anecdotes, will present themselves to us unsought! The difficulty will not be how to find subjects for our letter, but how to select from those that come crowding in upon our minds.

But all this implies, as we have already said, a careful and varied reading.

If the mind and heart dictate what should be said in a letter, good taste and refinement will lead us to observe the nice points laid down by the ceremonial regarding the mechanical part.

SECOND RULE.

WE SHOULD REFLECT ON WHAT WE ARE TO SAY.

Few rules are more important than this, because the mind and heart being both liable to be led away—the one by the desire to please, the other by affection—might tempt us to write things which would afterwards cause us serious inconvenience if not remorse.

Let us then weigh well every word we say, except when we are writing to friends, and *even then—* we shall not be on the spot to give an explanation, to rectify a misunderstanding, to clear up a doubt, and we may have reason to regret our precipitation. How many are there who imprudently commit to paper every report they hear, no matter how ill founded; every thought that enters their mind, forgetting that even *a word* may change a friend into a foe, and involve the refusal of an important request. *Reflection* is particularly necessary in *business* letters, and in those addressed to persons with whom we are but slightly acquainted. It is also essential when we are writing to those whom it would be injurious to our interests to prejudice against us.

As to the *mode* of reflecting, the best, indeed the only profitable way of doing so, at least for those who are very young and whose style is unformed, is to take up a pen for the purpose of writing, *not* the letter that is to be sent, but a copy of that letter.

Having written down what they wish to say, let them read it over calmly, modify its expressions, and curtail or add to them as the case may be. Finally, having thus revised, let them transcribe the letter.

For fairly educated persons such a course would not only be unnecessary, but would tend to destroy that ease of style which is one of the most desirable features of a well-written letter.

Another advantage of reflection is that it enables one to choose from the many thoughts that sometimes embarrass the mind, those that tend directly to the object one has in view.

THIRD RULE.

WE SHOULD NEVER FORGET OUR AGE OR POSITION.

This rule, which is founded on common sense, is obviously a most important one. It teaches that children or young persons should not arrogate to themselves the office of advising, correcting or censuring their seniors; that an inferior should not dictate to or lecture his superior; that the letters of those advanced in years should not savour of levity or frivolity.

It is true that these rules, like others, admit of exceptions, and in some cases may and ought to be swerved from. But good sense and politeness must always be our guide in the exceptional circumstances.

None but the giddy and the illiterate are likely to err against this rule. The impropriety of adopting a preaching tone cannot be too early impressed on the minds of children.

Few things are more graceful, nay original, in many instances than the letters of very young children. Why destroy all the freshness and charm of them by substituting for their artless prattle, set phrases and grave subjects. Grammatical errors should be pointed out to them. A child's ear is generally acute, and easily distinguishes between a correct and incorrect phrase, and this long before the intellect is sufficiently developed to understand the intricacies of the rules of syntax.

FOURTH RULE.

WE SHOULD REFLECT TO WHOM WE ARE WRITING.

To write a suitable letter nothing is more necessary than that we should fully realize who we are that write, and who the person is to whom we are writing.

It is this that regulates what should be said, and the way of saying it.

We should invariably make it a point to suit our style to the position of the person to whom we write.

Our judgment would be very much at fault were we to write as familiarly to a superior, an inferior, or a stranger, as we would to a relative or intimate friend.

The style must vary according to the subject of our letter. It would, for instance, be quite out of place to ask a favour or sue for forgiveness in such terms as one uses in giving directions.

We must all have learned from personal experience that the human heart is liable to fall an easy prey to vanity and susceptibility. Would we then avoid the danger of giving offence, let us imagine ourselves in the presence of the person whom we are about to address, and fashion our style accordingly.

Should a superior, for example, write inconsiderately and assume too authoritative a tone, his letter will fail to do good.

Let the style of an inferior be too abject, and he is despised and spurned. The least assumption of authority in an equal arouses the indignation of the person written to. Too much confidence in making a request is liable to be regarded as presumption ; excessive diffidence may be construed into pride.

When there is question of commending, or thanking another, we may perhaps write more freely, because in these cases we rarely incur the risk of hurting the feelings of the person concerned.

Yet while there are letters that really embarrass us, owing to the formality and thought they entail, how amply may we not indemnify ourselves in our correspondence with our relatives and friends !

True, here also we should call to mind whom we are writing to, and allow the heart to be our guide.

Friendship is expansive. It likes to be loquacious. Though it incessantly repeat the same ideas, trifles, *nothings*, still these repetitions possess an inexpressible charm both for the friend who writes and the friend to whom they are written.

Friendship desires confidence.

Feelings, ideas, hopes, projects—all may be included in letters of this kind.

It is easy to realize that a letter written with the conviction that the more one says the more

pleasure will be given, will impart a no ordinary
pleasure to the writer.

FIFTH RULE.

WE SHOULD NEVER WRITE ANYTHING PREJUDICIAL TO ANOTHER.

Of all the rules that could be laid down with
regard to letter-writing, there is none, perhaps, so
important as this. And yet, unfortunately, there is
none that is violated so frequently.

It is chiefly in correspondence between friends
that the failings of others are selected as a topic for
letters.

We imagine that our friend will not divulge the
contents of our letter; we have even requested of
him not to do so. But we may be quite sure that
he will not keep it secret, and sometimes our self-
love will have no objection to this.

'*Let there be no detractions in your letters,*'
wrote a celebrated author. '*Never under any
pretext let your pen echo the anecdotes more or less
malicious that circulate around you.*'

The wit that shines at the expense of others is
an unenviable gift, and the reputation it confers is
a stigma rather than an eulogium, particularly on a
woman.

We plead as an excuse that we mention it only
to a friend. But knowing, as we well do, the

instability of human friendships, are we quite sure
that the one in question will always last ?   Can
we be sure that this friend to whom we give our
confidence will always be worthy of it ?   'Treat
an enemy as if he were one day to be your friend,'
wrote a very wise man.   Would he have been less
wise had he added, 'Treat *most* friends as if they
were one day to be your enemies ' ?

How many are there who would willingly give
part of their fortunes not to have written, or to be
able to withdraw from those that possess them,
letters which compromise themselves, and many
others!

Let nothing therefore ever tempt us to write
anything unkind.

> ' For life is but a passing day,
>   No lip can tell how brief its span ;
> Then, oh, the little time we stay,
>   Let's speak of all the best we can.'

Again, we must never lose sight of this axiom.
' *Words fly away, but writing remains.*'

SIXTH RULE.

WE SHOULD WRITE AND SEND A LETTER AT 1H :
FITTING MOMENT.

To know how to avail one's self of ' *the favourable
opportunity* ' on every occasion, is one of the great

secrets of success in life. That the letter we write should be full of healthy, vigorous thought, gracefully and appropriately expressed, is no doubt to be desired; but no less desirable is it, of a surety, that our letter should reach its destination at the precise time when it can best exert all its possible influence for good. There is nothing more useful to the writer, nothing more gratifying to the recipient of a letter than this.

It is attention to this rule that induces a person who has a favour to ask, to select for doing so the day on which he who is to grant it has received good news.

It is this, likewise, that prevents our delaying a letter of condolence till after the expiration of the mourning, when our letter instead of pouring balm on the wound, would only re-open it.

Again, it is the observance of this rule that reminds us of the anniversary of a feast or birthday, and contrives to have our congratulations arrive at the appropriate moment—that admonishes us of the sufferings of a friend, and prompts us to send a word of sympathy and affection at the moment that he thinks himself forgotten.

It is this also that teaches us to defer a well-merited rebuke till tranquillity of mind is restored, and remorse has prepared the way for the lesson we intend to give.

But all this requires tact, reflection, an observant mind, a kind heart, and a firm and energetic will.

SEVENTH RULE.

WE SHOULD ANSWER EVERY LETTER WE RECEIVE.

Mere politeness requires that we answer every letter that requires a reply. To neglect to do so is to plead guilty to forgetfulness, contempt, or at least indifference. No lady or gentleman deserving the name ever allows a letter to remain unnoticed.

'But,' you will say, 'I have not time to answer every letter I receive.' To this we reply, 'Answer them nevertheless.'

Devote to this duty all the time it requires. Though your answer were to consist but of two words, write these two rather than leave the letter unreplied to.

The Qualities required in an Answer.

1. *It should be prompt,* particularly if it is to convey an opinion, advice, or consolation.

Those who consult us are always impatient for an answer. Why leave them in suspense? Perhaps our reply is of very great importance to them, and our silence disquiets or even irritates them. At all events, it cools their friendship. How many friendships have been broken off by neglect on this point? . . . And is not the preservation of a

2

friendship, however slight, worth the trifling trouble of sending a speedy answer?

Those whose lives are best regulated devote an hour every evening to acknowledging the letters received during the day. The only cases in which we are at liberty to defer sending an immediate answer, are when we have been asked to execute some commission, or procure information which of their own nature require delay. As politeness requires that our answer be as satisfactory as possible, we may postpone sending it till we have made the inquiries necessary to render it such.

2. *The answer should be complete.* That is, we must allude to everything asked in the letter received, consequently it would be well to read that letter over again immediately before replying to it. Etiquette requires *that we answer every question asked before touching on any other topic.*

As the impressions produced by the first perusal of a letter are generally the liveliest, and rarely recur to us on a second reading, it would be well to note them down on the letter according as they occur to us. This will prevent our forgetting anything we ought to say.

3. *An answer should be written calmly.* Although, as we have already remarked, we should note the letter received, still we should not answer it for some hours later, unless in particular cases.

When written, our letter should be read over carefully; and in the event of its having been penned by us whilst under the influence of excited feeling, it would be well to lay it aside till morning. If satisfied with it on a second perusal, it may be sent. Few things are more unwise than to write while smarting under the effects of some real or fancied wrong. Spoken recrimination or reproof is forgotten; but what we have once written down is irrevocable, and is often a source of subsequent regret.

As the poetess has it, using the license of her art, yet scarcely exaggerating:

> ' A moment, and my reckless ire
>   Had spent its fierce and lightning play ;
> But left a record of its fire
>   Too deeply scathed to pass away.'

If we would spare ourselves years, it may be, of anxiety and remorse, let us never send an angry letter, however great the provocation we may have received.

An answer being but the continuation in writing of a conversation begun in that way, it should be written in the same style as the letter that has elicited it. Thus if the letter received is sprightly, playful, the answer should be written in the same spirit. If it is serious, the reply should be serious. If affectionate, ours should be so likewise. If it tells of a favour conferred, the answer should be expressive of gratitude. If it contains a request, the

reply should be in acquiescence if possible; and **if**
unable to grant it, the refusal should be couched in
the kindest and most considerate terms.   Should
the letter be one of reproach, the reply should be a
frank acknowledgment of its being deserved, or a
calm explanation should the charge be groundless.

In the Second Part will be found some practical
hints on these subjects.

CHAPTER II.

RULES FOR THE STYLE OF LETTERS.

FIRST RULE.

WE SHOULD WRITE AS WE SPEAK.

A LETTER being but a substitute for verbal conversation, it should resemble it as much as possible.
The words should flow from our pen as from our
lips, without *apparent* effort, so that the reader
could not suppose that one word has been chosen in
preference to another.

It is scarcely necessary to say that this remark is
applicable only to those who are in the *habit of
speaking correctly.*   And, however well we may
speak, we should write still better; because what
is written remains, and is consequently open to criticism, while the spoken word passes with the moment.

Besides, we have time to collect and arrange our thoughts when writing, a thing by no means easy when speaking.

Hence it would be well to make a draft of such letters as are liable to be read beyond the home circle. This remark applies almost exclusively to the very young.

In a letter, as in conversation, we may pass rapidly from one subject to another, chatting on all kind of things. An anecdote may be told, a question discussed, an author quoted, a description given. In fact, the end we have in view is the only limit to be observed with regard to what is to be said in a letter, and the way of saying it.

In writing to those who are much our superiors or inferiors, we should use as few words as possible. In the former case, to take up too much of a great man's time is to take a liberty; in the latter, to be too diffuse is to be familiar. It is only in a correspondence with very intimate friends that long letters are permissible. If occasion necessitates a letter to a person very much occupied, one for instance absorbed in professional pursuits, politeness requires that it be as brief as is consistent with civility and perspicuity. It is unpardonable to take up people's time simply because we do not choose to be at the trouble of concentrating our thoughts and writing to the point.

SECOND RULE.

WE SHOULD WRITE NATURALLY.

Few things add a greater charm to a letter than that of its being natural.

To attain this end, over-fastidiousness in the choice of words, as well as the desire to shine, must be avoided.

If the words that first present themselves to us convey our ideas accurately, what need is there to seek for others ?   'In character, in manners, in style, in all things the supreme excellence is simplicity.'[1]

But simplicity of style must not be confounded with familiarity, which betrays itself by assuming a kind of equality not previously existing with those to whom we write, would be quite out of place in our correspondence with either superiors or inferiors. The former are often so punctilious about points of etiquette that the least infringement of its rules is liable to displease them, whilst inferiors are sometimes so sensitive that familiarity may seem to them contempt. A gentleman writing to a lady should never forget that her sex alone entitles her to his respect, and this even though he be her superior in rank.

[1] Longfellow.

It will contribute towards writing naturally and with graceful ease, to avoid the following faults :

1. *Long sentences.* 2. *Parenthesis.* 3. *Prolixity.*
4. *Ambiguity.* 5. *Affectation.*

Long sentences are not merely tiresome, but generally render the thought obscure and difficult to be understood. The shorter any sentence is, provided it is not abrupt, the better from the letter-writer's point of view. *Parentheses* divert the attention of the reader, and should therefore be avoided. *Prolixity, ambiguity,* and *affectation* either weary or irritate.

A natural style must not, however, be confused with a vulgar or even a homely one ; such as, for instance, '*I write to you at present.*' '*I take up my pen,*' etc.

No; a natural letter may be perfectly original, for, as we have already remarked, simplicity of style does not exclude all care. It certainly requires that everything savouring of pedantry be avoided ; but *negligence* can never be a virtue, even in our letters to our most intimate friends. It may be forgiven, but it cannot be excused.

An author compares a carelessly written letter to an unceremonious repast. The reader as well as the guest would prefer a little preparation to a sterile simplicity.

THIRD RULE.

WE MUST WRITE PERSPICUOUSLY.

'The first rule of all writing, that rule to which every other is subordinate, is that the words used by the writer shall be such as most fully and precisely convey his meaning."[1]   In other words, we should express ourselves so clearly that our reader may at a glance understand what we wish to say. To attain this, our letters must be free from all words of equivocal meaning, or open to different interpretations.

Two young girls, Miss L. and Miss H., being about to leave school before the distribution of prizes, Miss L., who lived in the country, asked Miss H. to write to inform her as to whether any prize should be awarded her, that she might go and fetch it.   On the appointed day she received the following note:

'*Miss H. has the honour to inform Miss L. that she has obtained the first prize for history.*'

Elated by her success, Miss. L. repairs to the distribution hall.   But alas! the premium is for her friend.   Filled with indignation the disappointed candidate flies in search of her companion, shows her her note, and taxes her with having deceived her.

[1] Lord Macaulay.

'What!' exclaims Miss H., 'did I not tell you it was *I* that won the prize ?'

A second perusal of the note showed that it might apply to either. *It was not clear.*

The note should have run thus:

'Miss H. has the honour to inform Miss L. that she, Miss H., has won the first prize for history.'

FOURTH RULE.

WE SHOULD WRITE CORRECTLY AND LEGIBLY.

This rule requires that we never allow a word of incorrect spelling to glide into our letters.

Formerly, owing to the backward state of education, or the looseness of the science, faults of this kind were excusable. But in this age of intellectual culture they are unpardonable.

To write legibly means that we are to write a clear, fair hand, 'that those who run may read.' In a busy age like the present, when everyone's time has a certain value, we have no right to impose the reading of hieroglyphics on our correspondents. Capitals should be used in the proper places, *i*'s dotted, *t*'s crossed, and only the most obvious abbreviations indulged in.'

To write so rapidly as not to allow ourselves time to form our letters, denotes a want of politeness or self-possession.

Egotism, or *stupidity,* is the characteristic that the analyst discovers in illegible writing.

The observance of this fourth rule applies particularly to signatures, which should be as simple and unostentatious as possible.[1] 'Nothing is more absurd than to see a person whose name can have no significance to the world in general, sign himself at least as elaborately as if he were the premier.'

All flourishes should be avoided, and an extreme simplicity be the distinctive feature of all writing. As we have already remarked, simplicity *in everything* is almost invariably characteristic of the refined and cultured. Should we be unable to write straight without a transparency, we may use one; but none except *very young children* should ever *line* their letters.

FIFTH RULE.

Hints as to Abbreviations.

We must, as much as possible, avoid abbreviations, or the omission of letters, particularly in writing to superiors.

In commercial correspondence, abbreviations may be adopted for the sake of saving time.[2]

---

[1] Instances have occurred of persons having been obliged to cut off the signature and gum it on to the envelope containing the reply. But this example should not be followed, except in cases where it is really impossible to decipher the writing.

[2] A merchant wishing to know whether there was any news, sent his correspondent a sheet of paper with only a note of interrogation on it. The latter, emulating the laconic style of his master, replied by a zero !

The titles 'Capt.,' 'Esq.,' and ' Dr.,' are written thus by the most punctilious.

The name should always be written *in full* at the end of our letters. Some have an absurd habit of omitting their surname; and we sometimes find a letter signed 'Mary' or 'Harry,' without having the remotest idea as to the identity of its writer. Of course this remark does not apply to those who are nearly related, such as are the members of a family.

SIXTH RULE.

WE SHOULD WRITE ELEGANTLY.

It must not be supposed that elegance of style is incompatible with simplicity. The reverse of this is the case ; for the more elegant a letter is, the more natural it is. Simplicity of style, as we have already explained, is a freedom from affectation, whilst elegance is that something which enables us to express ourselves in such a way as to please and fascinate without its being perceptible that we had this object in view.

A letter is a substitute for ourselves. Being unable to pay a visit, we depute this in our stead, and should therefore adorn it as we would adorn ourselves.

Now there is, first, an *official dress*, which, though not perhaps the most elegant, is irreproachable under

every point of view, as being laid down by custom
There are also *official* letters, in which certain set
forms are to be observed, and of these we will speak
later on. Then there is a *becoming* costume which
we wear when visiting a friend. Our aim is not
to dazzle, but *to please ;* and actuated by this feeling, we instinctively select the dress and ornaments
most likely to accomplish this end without directly
proposing it to ourselves.

So is it likewise with our letter when its only
object is *to gratify* or *to do good* to the person to
whom it is addressed. We take up our pen, and
almost intuitively an anecdote, a simile, a witticism,
a reminiscence, a touching allusion, a kind word, a
delicate compliment, suggests itself.

Very big words should be avoided. The use of
interjections, such as ' *Oh,*' ' *Ah,*' etc., are absolutely
opposed to elegance of style, as savouring too much
of affectation.

CHAPTER III.

Rules for the Ceremonial of Letters.

By the ceremonial of letters is meant certain rules
which custom has laid down, and which all well-
bred persons have adopted. They are as follow :

FIRST RULE.

WE SHOULD COMPLY WITH THE ESTABLISHED CUSTOMS.

These customs are based on the mutual respect that we owe to one another. They are, it is true, mere exterior marks of ceremony, and may even mean nothing in themselves; still, they always possess the significance which one wishes to attach to them.

These customs are universally followed by those whose rank or education entitle them to be regarded as criterions in matters of this kind; and as they contain nothing repugnant to good sense or good taste, we must comply with them if we would not incur the reproach of *ignorance* or *levity*, two faults more prejudicial to us than it is generally supposed. If the *style* of a letter displays the genius of the writer, the *ceremonial* of it discloses the still more desirable qualities of refinement and kindness.

To refuse to comply with these usages is *to despise the wisdom of others.* It is to accustom one's self to the spirit of independence, which begins by shaking off the yoke in trifles and ends by breaking the fetters of essential duties. It is *to fail in respect* to those who have a right to receive it from us.

SECOND RULE.

We should be Acquainted with all the Received Customs.

These consist chiefly of what follows, viz. :
The paper ;
The title, and place for the title, of the person to whom we write ;
The margin ;
The date ;
The ending ;
The signature ;
The postscript ;
The folding of the letter ;
The envelope ;
The postage ;
The seal ; and lastly,
The punctuation.
We will now give a brief explanation of all that is necessary to be known on each of these points.

THE PAPER.

I. The Size of the Paper.

There are the *large,* the *middle,* and the *small sizes.*
The large, or, as it is generally called, *letter-paper,* is reserved for petitions to Government, etc.

The *middle* or *ordinary* size note-paper is used on nearly every occasion. It is on this we should always write to superiors.

The *small* or Albert size may be used for *short* business letters. We should never write on a half sheet; to do so would evince either carelessness, contempt, or penuriousness, particularly now that paper is so cheap.

We should never *cross* our letters. If they are very long, there is nothing to prevent our using as many additional sheets as we require, but we should *page* them, so that the reader may see at a glance what sheets follow each other.

It would be to sin against politeness, against good feeling even, to reply to a note that one has received *on the reverse of the written side*. Nothing could justify our *returning part of the writing sent us*, save perhaps the fact of being shipwrecked on a desert island, where the commodity could not be got at. To act thus under ordinary circumstances could hardly fail of being regarded as an insult.

II. Colour of the Paper.

At present every colour is used, but the more delicate the tints the better, as very deep shades are liable to look vulgar.

Perhaps, on the whole, *good* white paper is the most elegant. This, however, is a matter of taste.

III. Mourning Paper.

'The paper and envelope should have a black border, suitable to the degree of relationship to the dead, and the length of time one has been in mourning.

'*Even in the very deepest mourning,*exaggerations of black border are unbecoming and out of taste. Real grief is always unostentatious.'

IV. Perfume on Paper.

Few things are more at variance with the usages of good society than that of using perfume on paper.

The odour of Russia leather is an exception to this rule, and letters or papers kept in desks of this description will imbibe its perfume.

V. Stamps and Crests on Paper.

An administration, business, or educational house may have its name printed on the left side, on the top of the sheet; but this stamp should be simple, clear, and perfectly legible.

'If monograms and crests are used in ordinary correspondence, they should be as simple as possible, and in one colour only. Gilt monograms and crests printed in a variety of colours are pretentious.'

Monograms should never appear but on the best paper. Cheap finery is never in taste.

Crests, arms, etc., can be tolerated only when they are above suspicion. Thackeray has many a laugh at the blazoned arms of the '*nouveau riche.*'

"Ladies, whether married or unmarried, are not entitled to either crests or mottoes."[1] But, though not entitled to crests, courtesy authorizes married ladies to use their husbands' crests, or, if unmarried, their fathers'.

Symbolic flowers on the paper are absurd, except in the case of little children.

VI. NEATNESS OF THE PAPER.

No letter should contain erasures or blots under any circumstance whatever. Neither should there be any supplying of omitted words, unless we are on very intimate terms with our correspondent.

Should the least blot or speck get on the letter we should write it over again, rather than send it thus.

We should never defer writing a letter to post-hour. 'Post off,' is the conclusion to many a careless and ill-advised letter. Hurried work is seldom good work.

THE MARGIN.

Formerly the margin was marked either by a crease in the paper or by a pencil line. Nowadays,

---

[1] Sir J. Bernard Burke, Ulster King-at-Arms.

though the margin is still left, it is no longer traced out. The margin should always be proportioned to the size of our paper. If that be large, the margin must be pretty wide. If the paper be small, the margin must be narrow. We should carefully avoid encroaching on the space set apart for it, as any un-evenness in the lines spoils the neatness of the letter.

There should not be *two* margins, as they cramp the writer, and are altogether out of date since note-paper has been narrowed to its present limits.

THE DATE OF THE DAY ON WHICH THE LETTER IS WRITTEN.

It is always well to date our letters. As to those on business, this is absolutely necessary, the omission of a date being sufficient to invalidate the most important letter. Every business letter should be dated on the top of the sheet, at the right-hand side, and immediately under the address. With regard to other letters there is no decided rule. It is generally written to the left, a little below the signature.

THE ENDINGS OF LETTERS.

A celebrated writer says that the part of a letter which cost him most was its two last lines.

The reason of this is that it is in these lines we are most likely to wound the susceptibility of those to whom we write, should they seem wanting in the deference or cordiality they look for. 'Faithfully yours,' from a superior. 'Yours truly' or 'sincerely yours,' from an equal. 'Your obedient servant,' from an inferior—are the forms generally used.

Let it be remembered, however, that a friendly letter is a conversation between friends. Surely then the 'good-bye' at the end should be something more than a mere formality. Gay, sad, affectionate, sympathetic—whatever the letter has been, *that* the end should be especially. Last impressions are strongest : a *chill* there, and the warmest letter will seem cold.

THE SIGNATURE OF LETTERS.

The place for the signature is at the right-hand side.

It should be accompanied by our address, including the *post town*, if we are writing to strangers.

Young persons should pay particular attention to the above remark, as they are very apt to neglect giving the name of their post town, and the result is that their letters must needs remain unanswered. *Nothing should ever induce us to write an anonymous letter.* Kemp says, speaking on this subject: "Of all detestable things, this is the most odious. Friend may censure friend, foe vent his spleen, but let it never be done under the cover of anonymous writing. What dear ties have been either sundered or loosened by this fiend of mischief; what hopes of love blighted, what deeds of charity delayed, what virtues sullied by this foul invisible spirit! Friendships over which time could exercise no control, which distance or poverty could not shake or alter, have been for ever chilled by suspicion, or completely destroyed by anonymous malice. Neither shall they be completely guiltless who believe these secret calumniators of a man's character. Burn then these unauthorized epistles. Look for the signature before you glance at the matter, and thus this enemy of plain dealing (for such is the anonymous correspondent) will be foiled in his attempt to pervert innocence, and your own bosom will have the satisfaction of thinking well of those whom this demon of mischief would destroy."

THE POSTSCRIPT.

This word, which signifies something written (*scriptum*) after (*post*), and refers to whatever is added after the signature, should be prefixed by the letters P.S. Originally the postscript was written to supply something which had been omitted, and thus save the time that would be necessary to re-write the letter. But by degrees it has become so general, so important even, that it is said if we wish to find the *real* subject of the letter, we must look for it in the postscript. This applies particularly to ladies' letters. But this is absurd. Very often a postscript shows only a levity that has forgotten something that should be said, or a sloth that shrinks from the trouble of writing the letter again.

A postscript is never allowable in letters to superiors.

THE FOLDING OF THE LETTER.

The letter should always be folded to suit the size of the envelope. If that is square, the paper is to be merely doubled in two. If the envelope is long and narrow, the paper may be folded in three. In every instance the letter should be measured with the cover that is to contain it, and thus prevent unnecessary creases, which invariably give it a slovenly appearance.

It would be well to have a supply of different-sized envelopes in our desk to suit the note-paper.

THE ENVELOPES.

They should be of thick paper, to prevent the writing from appearing through them.

THE ADDRESS.

The address, which should be written very legibly, is to give the name, surname, and title of the person to whom we write.

It should begin to the left, and more than half-way up the envelope, particularly if it is to be a long address of many lines.

If the person to whom the letter is addressed be the guest of another, the host's name should follow before the name of the house. On this point custom is now imperative. Some put 'C/o,' 'Kind care

of,' etc., 'At so-and-so's.' Though all these forms are
usual, still they may be, and are, correctly dispensed
with, the host's name following simply on that of
the person for whom it is intended.

DIRECTIONS FOR ADDRESSING PERSONS OF ALL RANKS.

THE ROYAL FAMILY.

To the Queen's Most Excellent Majesty—Most
Gracious Sovereign, May it please your Majesty.

Conclude—I remain (or, I have the honour to
remain), with the profoundest veneration (or, respect), Madam (or, Sire), your Majesty's most
faithful subject and dutiful servant.

To His Royal Highness the Prince of Wales—
Sir, May it please your Royal Highness.

Conclude—I remain, Sir (or, Madam), with the
utmost (or, greatest) respect, your Royal Highness's
most dutiful and most obedient servant.

In the same manner to the rest of the Royal
Family.

Conclude—I have the honour to remain, Sir (or,
Madam), with great respect, your Highness's most
obedient servant.

TO THE NOBILITY.

To his Grace the Duke of S.—My Lord Duke ;
or, May it please your Grace ; or, Your Grace.

Conclude—I have the honour to be, My Lord Duke (or, My Lady), your Grace's most devoted (or most obedient and humble) servant.

To the Most Noble the Marquis of B.—My Lord Marquis, your Lordship.

Conclude—I have the honour to be, My Lord Marquis, your Lordship's (or, Madam, your Ladyship's) most obedient and humble servant.

To the Right Honourable the Earl of B.—My Lord, your Lordship.

Conclude—I have the honour to be, My Lord, your Lordship's (or, My Lady, your Ladyship's) most obedient humble servant.

To the Right Honourable the Lord Viscount D. —My Lord, your Lordship.

To the Right Honourable the Lord F.—My Lord, your Lordship.

Conclude—I have the honour to be, My Lord, your Lordship's (or, My Lady, your Ladyship's) most obedient and humble servant.

Ladies are addressed according to the rank of their husbands.

Widows of Noblemen are addressed in the same style, the word *Dowager* being added. To the Most Noble the Dowager Marchioness of G——.

The sons of Dukes, Marquises, and the eldest sons of Earls, have by courtesy the title of Lord and Right Honourable; and the title of Lady is given to their daughters.

The younger sons of Earls, and sons of Viscounts and Barons, are styled Esquires, and Honourable, and all their daughters Honourable.

The title of Honourable is likewise conferred on such persons as have the Queen's Commission, and upon those gentlemen who enjoy places of trust and honour.

The title of Right Honourable is given to no Commoner, excepting those who are Members of Her Majesty's Most Honourable Privy Council, and the three Lord Mayors of London, York, and Dublin, and the Lord Provost of Edinburgh, during the time they are in office.

TO THE CLERGY.

To His Eminence the Most Reverend Edward Cardinal Preston, Archbishop of D.—May it please your Eminence, or, My Lord Cardinal.

Conclude—I remain with the deepest respect, My Lord Cardinal, your Eminence's most obedient servant.

To the Most Reverend Dr. Greer, Lord Archbishop of C.—My Lord, or, Your Grace.

To the Right Reverend Dr. Wheewell, Lord Bishop of M.—My Lord.

Conclude—I remain with the highest respect, My Lord Archbishop, your Grace's most devoted servant. I have the honour to be, My Lord Bishop, your Lordship's most humble servant.

The Very Reverend the Dean of C.—Mr.

Dean.—The Venerable Archdeacon of F., etc.—Very Reverend Sir, etc.

Conclude—I have the honour to be, Very Reverend Sir (or, Mr. Dean or Mr. Archdeacon) your most obedient servant.

To the Very Reverend Alfred Canon M., P.P., B.

All Rectors, Vicars, Curates, Lecturers, and Clergymen of other inferior denominations, are styled Reverend.

THE HOUSES OF PARLIAMENT.

The House of Lords.

To the Right Honourable the Lords Spiritual and Temporal of the United Kingdom of Great Britain and Ireland in Parliament assembled—My Lords, or, May it please your Lordships.

Conclude—I have the honour to be, My Lords, your Lordships' most obedient and humble servant.

The House of Commons.

To the Honourable the Commons of the United Kingdom of Great Britain and Ireland in Parliament assembled—Gentlemen, or, May it please your Honourable House.

Conclude—I have the honour to be, Gentlemen, your most obedient humble servant.

To the Right Honourable C. W. C., Speaker of the House of Commons—who is generally one of Her Majesty's Most Honourable Privy Council—Sir, or Mr. Speaker.

Conclude—I have the honour to be, Sir, your most obedient servant.

A member of the House of Commons not ennobled:—

To Hugh B——., Esq., M.P.—Sir.

Conclude—I have the honour to be your most obedient servant.

To the Officers of Her Majesty's Household.

They are for the most part addressed according to their rank and quality, though sometimes agreeably to the nature of their office; as, My Lord Steward, My Lord Chamberlain, Mr. Vice-Chamberlain, etc.; and in all superscriptions of letters which relate to gentlemen's employments, their style of office should never be omitted. If they have more offices than one, only the highest need be mentioned.

To the Officers of the Army and Navy.

In the Army all Noblemen are styled according to their rank, to which is added their employ.

To the Hon. A. B——., Esq., Lieutenant-General, Major-General, Brigadier-General of Her Majesty's Forces—Sir, or, Your Honour.

To the Right Honourable the E. of S., Captain of Her Majesty's First Troop of Horse Guards,

Band of Gentlemen-Pensioners, Band of Yeomen
of the Guards, etc.—My Lord, or, Your Lordship.

All Colonels are styled Honourable ; all inferior
Officers should have the name of their employment
set first; as, for example, to Major Wilton Harding,
to Captain Hubert St. Clair.

In the Navy, all Admirals are styled Honourable,
and Noblemen according to quality and office. The
other Officers as in the Army.

To Ambassadors, Secretaries, and Consuls.

All Ambassadors have the title of Excellency
added to their quality, as have also Plenipotentiaries,
Foreign Governors, and the Lord Lieutenants and
Lord Justices of Ireland.

To his Excellency Sir B—— C——, Baronet, Her
Britannic Majesty's Envoy Extraordinary, Minister
and Plenipotentiary to the Ottoman Porte—Sir,
or, Your Excellency.

To his Excellency E. F., Esq., Ambassador to Her
Most Christian Majesty—Sir, or, Your Excellency.

To his Excellency the Baron de A., His Prussian
Majesty's Resident at the Court of Great Britain
—Sir, or, Your Excellency.

To the Judges and Lawyers.

All the Judges, if Privy Councillors, are styled
Right Honourable; as, for instance:

To the Right Honourable A. B., Lord High

Chancellor of Great Britain—My Lord, or, Your Lordship.

To the Right Honourable P. V., Master of the Rolls—Sir, or, Your Honour.

To the Right Honourable Sir G. L., Lord Chief Justice of the Queen's Bench, or of the Common Pleas—My Lord, or, Your Lordship.

To the Honourable A. B., Lord Chief Baron—Sir, or, May it please you, Sir.

To the Right Honourable A. D., Esq., one of the Justices, or, To Judge M.—Sir, or, May it please you, Sir.

To Sir R. D., Her Majesty's Attorney, Solicitor, or Advocate-General—Sir.

All others in the Law, according to the offices and rank they bear, every Barrister having the title of Esquire given him.

To the Lieutenancy and Magistracy.

To the Right Honourable G., Earl of C., Lord Lieutenant and Custos Rotulorum of the County of Durham—My Lord, or, Your Lordship.

To the Right Honourable T. S., Esq., Lord Mayor of the City of London, My Lord, or, Your Lordship.

All Gentlemen in the Commission of the Peace have the title of Esquire and Worshipful, as have also all Sheriffs and Recorders.

The Aldermen and Recorders of London are

styled Right Worshipful, as are all Mayors of Corporations, except Lord Mayors.

To A. B., Esq., High Sheriff of the County of York—Sir, or, Your Worship.

To the Right Worshipful W. D., Esq., Alderman of Tower Ward, London—Sir, or, Your Worship.

To the Right Honourable J. A., Recorder of the City of London—Sir, or, Your Worship.

The Governors of Hospitals, Colleges, etc., which consist of Magistrates, or have any such among them, are styled Right Worshipful, or Worshipful, as their titles allow.

To the Governors of the Crown.

To his Excellency the Duke of R., Lord Lieutenant of Ireland—My Lord, or, Your Excellency.

To the Right Honourable Lord N., Governor of Dover Castle, etc.—My Lord, or, Your Lordship.

The second Governors of Colonies, appointed by the Queen, are called Lieutenant-Governors.

To Incorporate Bodies.

To the Honourable the Governors, Deputy-Governors, and Directors of the Bank of England—Your Honours.

To the Masters and Wardens of the Worshipful Company of Mercers—Your Worships.

THE POSTAGE.

Politeness demands that we put on the full number of stamps required for the postage of a letter. If we are in doubt as to the weight of our letter, and are unable to ascertain it, we should *over-stamp* it rather than incur the risk of subjecting its recipient to even the most trifling fine.

Etiquette does not oblige us to stamp such letters as are answers to business letters of inquiry from strangers; still, even in cases of this kind, it would be better to do so, as one is rarely a loser by politeness.

Custom authorizes our enclosing a stamped envelope with our address, to persons with whom we have no relations, and from whom we require an answer; but this should never be done to persons of rank.

The stamp should be placed exactly in the right-hand corner of the envelope; it should not be turned upside down or slanting, as carelessness even in trifles takes from the elegance of a letter, and evinces a rudeness to the person to whom we are writing.

THE SEAL.

Gummed envelopes are now generally used. But all official letters and private communications should be sealed with wax—the official because they should bear the arms of the writer, those of a private nature because the gummed envelopes may be easily opened, and the contents of our letter become public.

In the event of wax becoming blackened by smoke, it would be well to move the stick of lighted wax on the drops we have let fall on the envelope.

If the impression be indistinct we must drop more wax on the envelope, and again set the seal on it.

The wax should be stamped with a seal bearing the crest or initials of the writer, but never on any account should it bear the impress of a coin, medal, or thimble.

Devices and emblems on seals, though formerly very fashionable, are now rarely used. Still they are not contrary to good taste, provided there be no want of judgment in the selection of them.

The celebrated Madame de Sévigné had for her device a swallow on the wing, with the motto 'Le froid me chasse.'[1]

That of Madame Lafayette consisted of a pigeon, bearing a letter with the words 'Plus heureuse que moi, elle restera près de toi.'[2]

On the whole, perhaps, emblems savour a little of affectation and sentimentality; still, as we have already said, if well chosen, we may use them without any breach of etiquette.

POST-CARDS.

Post-cards are now generally used for giving orders to business houses, acknowledging the receipt

[1] 'Coldness alienates me.'
[2] 'More fortunate than I, it will remain with thee.'

of parcels, asking and giving information concerning an invalid, etc.

As they are liable to be read by everyone, *nothing of a private* nature should ever be written on them.

Clearness, conciseness, and courtesy should be the distinguishing features of post-cards.

A disagreeable message should never be sent on them. It adds to the annoyance of bad news that it should be cheap. If ' brevity is the soul of wit,' a post-card may be witty. The 'outward flourishes' have no place there. Swift, Pope, Burns, Moore, would doubtless have written post-card messages, and famous ones, but Dr. Johnson could not, any more than the great living patron of political post-cards, have made anything but a ridiculous figure on such a small sheet, and at such an undignified price.

PUNCTUATION.

The following rules from Nichol's 'Primer of Composition,' may not be considered extraneous matter. They will, doubtless, add to the usefulness of this little work.

" The relation of the parts of a sentence to one another should be made as plain as possible by proper arrangement: but it is sometimes made more clear in spoken language by proper pauses, and in written or printed language by PUNCTUATION.

"The following are the points common in English, and the main rules for their use :—

"1. The FULL STOP (.), or Period, marks the close of a sentence, whether simple or complex, loose or periodic. It indicates that the construction is complete, and that an assertion has been fully made; though other sentences in the same paragraph may follow to modify the thought. The period is also employed to mark abbreviations, as in Christian names or titles—T. B. Potter; Lord Beaconsfield, K.G.

"2. The COLON (:) generally indicates that the sentence might grammatically be regarded as finished, but that something follows without which the full force of the remark would be lost: 'Study to acquire a habit of thinking: no study is more important.' This point is used after a general statement followed by the specification of two or more heads: 'Three properties belong to wisdom: nature, learning, and experience.' A direct quotation is often introduced by a colon: 'He was heard to say: "I have done with the world."'

"3. The SEMICOLON (;) is used similarly, but it indicates a closer connection in the clause that follows. Reasons are preceded by semicolons: 'Economy is no disgrace; for it is better to live on a little than to outlive a great deal.' So are clauses in opposition, when the second is introduced by an adversative. 'Straws swim at the surface;

4

but pearls lie at the bottom.' Without the adversative, prefer a colon : 'Prosperity showeth vice : adversity virtue.' Several members dependent on a common clause follow semicolons : *e.g.*, ' Philosophers assert that nature is unlimited; that her treasures are endless; that the increase of knowledge will never cease.'

" 4. The COMMA (,) represents the shortest natural pause in reading or speaking the sentence. It groups the words immediately related in grammar or sense, and indicates where their connection is interrupted. There is considerable latitude in the use of commas. Avoid using them lavishly ; mere adjective or adverbial phrases do not require them. The following, for instance, needs none :—

"'By carefully pandering to the passions of the half-educated mob you will hardly fail to secure their votes.'

" But this does :—

"' By pandering to the passions of the mob, who in this part of the country control the elections, you will secure their votes.'

" Some special uses of the comma are worthy of note. It is employed—

" (*a*) To separate adjectives in opposition but closely connected :—

'Though deep, yet clear.'

" (*b*) After adjectives, nouns and verbs, in compound sentences, where 'and' is omitted :—

"'Are all thy conquests, glories, triumphs, spoils, shrunk to this little measure ?'

"'He fills, he bounds, connects, and equals all.'

"So with pairs of words :—

"'Old and young, rich and poor, wise and foolish, were involved in the ruin of the Glasgow Bank.'

"Similarly, to separate a series of assertions relating to the same nominative and not connected by a conjunction :—

"'He rewarded his friends, chastised his foes, set Justice on her seat and made his conquest secure.'

"(c) Before a qualifying clause introduced by a relative :—

"'Peace at any price, which these orators seem to advocate, means war at any cost.'

"Note that a relative clause not necessary to the antecedent must be marked off by commas; thus :

"'Sailors, who are generally superstitious, say it is unlucky to embark on a Friday.'

"When the clause is an essential part of the antecedent only one comma is used :—

"'The sailor who is not superstitious, will embark on any day.' The adjective is followed by a comma because the nominative 'sailor' is not immediately followed by the verb.

"(d) When the nominative is a clause, a comma is often placed after it.

"'That he had persistently disregarded every warning and persevered in his reckless course, had not yet undermined his credit with his dupes.'

"(e) On both sides of an explanatory clause, without which the sentence would be verbally complete :—

"'The shield was oblong, four feet in length and two in breadth, and was guarded by plates of brass.'

"'The coast, as far as we have been able to explore it, is rocky.'

"(f) After an address:—'My son, give me thy heart.'

"(g) After the adverbs—nay, however, finally, at least, etc.

"'Finally, let me sum up the argument.'

"(h) After a nominative, where the verb is under-derstood :—

"'To err is human; to forgive, divine.'

"The importance of accuracy in the use of the comma is illustrated by the different meaning which its insertion at one place or another may give to such sentences as the following:

"'You will be rich if you be industrious in a few years.'

"Lord George Sackville, on trial for an alleged offence, was accused of contempt of court for making an ambiguous pause in saying:

"'I stand here as a prisoner unfortunately that gentleman sits there as my judge.'

"In the latter instance, however, the ambiguity was perhaps intentional, and it is to be observed that where so much depends on a point, there is commonly some fault in the construction of the sentence. As a rule, beware of relying on the punctuation to indicate the sense: it ought to appear from the words chosen and from their arrangement.

"5. The POINT OF INTERROGATION (?) is used after questions put by the writer, or questions reported directly:

"'He said, "When do you mean to come back ?"'

"It should not be used when the question is reported indirectly:

"'He asked me when I intended to return.'

"6. The POINT OF EXCLAMATION (!), used after apostrophes or expressions of violent emotion; should rarely appear in ordinary prose. It is quite out of place in narrative or historical composition, e.g. 'Hurrah for Argyle at last! From this time forth he is openly a Covenanter.'

"7. The same remark applies to the PARENTHESIS ( ), or the still more abrupt break indicated by the DASH (——). It has been fairly observed that these signs are often a mere cover for the writer's ignorance of the points: they are, however, admissible when a clause is obviously thrust in, and has less connection with the rest of the sentence than would be indicated by commas, as:

"'He gained from heaven ('twas all he wished), a friend.'

"'Fame is the spur that the clear spirit doth raise (That last infirmity of noble mind), To scorn delights, and live laborious days.'

"The following is a good example of the proper employment of the dash :

"'At the last stage—what is its name ? I have forgotten in seven-and-thirty years—there is an inn with a little green and trees before it.'

"A colon with a dash after it (:—) frequently introduces a quotation, especially when given as an instance or example.

"8. A shorter line (-) called the HYPHEN is used—

"(a) To connect parts of a word divided at the end of a line. Remember to take care that you divide words according to the component parts of their derivation :—anti-dote; not an-tidote; consult, not cons-ult.

"(b) To connect two or more nouns, adjectives, or particles, so as to form them into a single compound, as—'Dry-as-dust history;' 'That never-to-be-forgotten day;' 'That man-monkey.' Such compounds should be used sparingly.

"9. The marks (" ") should be employed wherever a quotation is made, or a speech directly reported. In dramatic dialogue, however, they are omitted, it being taken for granted that the words are in the mouths of imaginary speakers.

"10. CONTRACTIONS.—The following signs are universally recognised :

"*i.e.*, for *id est*, that is to say, to expand or explain; *e.g.*, for *exempli gratiâ*, for example's sake, to illustrate.

" *Viz.*, for *videlicet*, to wit, to give an instance or enumerate the parts before referred to generally.

" *Etc.*, for *etcetera*, and the rest, when all the parts necessary to illustrate the proposition have been named, and it would be waste of time to complete the catalogue.

" ⌃, for *insert*. Cobbett calls this sign ' the blunder mark.'

" (') The apostrophe before the s of the possessive, and to mark contractions or elisions—

'Nought's got, all's spent

When our desire is had without content.'

" This latter use should be mainly confined to poetry.

" 11. CAPITALS are properly employed to mark :

" The first word of a sentence, or of a line of verse.

" The first word of a direct quotation.

" The first personal pronoun I, and the interjection O.

" Proper names, high titles, and names of the Deity.

" Very emphatic words, and names of personified objects.

" 12. ITALICS are admissible to emphasize. They are of frequent and hardly avoidable occurrence in short treatises, to mark a portion of a sentence or paragraph to which special attention has to be called. But in ordinary writing the fewer italics we use the better."[1]

---

[1] Editors of Reviews are very severe upon authors who indulge in italics.

SECOND PART.

DIFFERENT KINDS OF LETTERS.

ALL letters may be classed under three heads:

1. *Friendly* or *familiar letters.*
2. *Letters of courtesy.*
3. *Business letters.*

In friendly letters the heart must be our guide, as being the source whence they emanate.

Letters of courtesy are those in which the intellect predominates. Not alone does etiquette require us to write these letters, but it dictates also that they be written after a particular form, which is more or less laid down by custom.

Business letters include all those which have for their end our worldly interests or projects.

A few hints regarding the three classes of letters indicated above, may not be altogether useless to the young, for the formation of whose taste and judgment this little work is chiefly designed.

They should be taught that one can and ought to express one's self *tersely*, *simply*, and *politely*.

CHAPTER I.

GENERAL ADVICE.

I. FRIENDLY LETTERS.

IN this class is comprised not merely the letters to our relatives and friends, but also such as are addressed to those for whom our veneration equals our affection. For friendly letters there are no particular rules. They are the dictates of the heart, and *that*, however deficient in worldly culture, knows what to say and how to say it most effectively. Not alone does it avoid all that could give pain, but it contrives to invest everything it says with an inexpressible charm. The polished phrase and rounded sentence may, it is true, be wanting, but the loss is more than compensated for by the genial accents of friendship or esteem. This class of letters is by far the easiest to write. But this remark refers solely to such as owe their origin to genuine friendship, and is not applicable to those only written through politeness.

A young girl, having to write a formal letter, copied one of those found in a '*Letter Writer*.' 'Turn over the page,' wrote her friend the next day, 'and you will find my answer.' True, she gave her friend a salutary lesson, but failed herself in politeness. Good-breeding dictates that we should not appear to notice the mistakes of others.

When writing to a friend we should never consult books as to what we are to say. Let us speak *our own* thoughts and feelings, and there can be but little doubt that, however unpretending our style, our letters will at least be fully equal to those found in the insipid collections edited for the illiterate and the idle. Few second-hand articles are of much value—but a second-hand letter is of none at all. Is there not a mine of feeling within us from which to draw affection, gratitude, esteem, as the case may be? We are not true to our better selves when we fail to turn to this source.

There should be no restrictions as to the length of friendly letters. We have already remarked with a celebrated author that *friendship* is *expansive*. We may add with another writer: " Our letter is eloquent when the heart is its guide."

The pen of friendship consoles, encourages, advises, reproves, leads towards God. It has a thousand ways of saying '*A happy New Year*'—of wishing a happy feast; it constantly repeats, yet never says the same thing. It seems to have but two phrases at its disposal, 'I love you' and 'I thank you;' and under its spell these simple words grow into long sentences which one never tires of reading.

II. LETTERS OF COURTESY.

Under the title of letters of courtesy may be classed all those which politeness or the duties of our position oblige us to write. Thus an official should—

1st. Congratulate his superior in the event of the latter receiving promotion.

2nd. He should thank him for any favour or patronage conferred by him directly or through his influence.

3rd. He should write to wish him a happy Christmas or birthday.

Letters of explanation, of excuse and the like, as well as those of condolence, invitation and their answers, circulars, etc., are all included under the heading of *letters of courtesy.*

The general characteristics of letters of this class are an easy politeness and elegance which can only be acquired by reading and a knowledge of the customs of society.

As the intellect has more share than the heart in letters of this kind, those whose style is unformed would do well when about to write any letter of mere ceremony, to copy before transcribing it.

So difficult on some occasions is the composition of letters of this class, that one whose fame in the epistolary art is of European celebrity, has graphically described it as '*ploughing on paper.*'

We will speak more in detail of them in the following chapter.

III. BUSINESS LETTERS.

Under this heading may be classed all communications that regard the details of life.

Petitions, requests, recommendations, commercial correspondence, directions given to a servant regarding household matters, commissions to a friend or to an inferior, etc., fall under this category.

The general characteristics of business letters should be *terseness* and *conciseness*.

Terseness, which conveys in the clearest possible way and fewest possible words what we wish to say.

Conciseness, which dispenses with all exaggerated forms of drawing-room politeness, and enters at once into the business in hand, passing without delay from one subject to another. If we can express what we want to say in four words, let us not write fifty under pretence of courtesy. The briefer a business letter is the better. One may be very polished in a few words.

With regard to business letters to our inferiors we should, while avoiding all that could savour of arrogance, abstain from familiarity.

A lady, for instance, should not address her milliner as '*My dearest Friend*,' that form being only allowable between equals, and not even between them unless they are on very intimate terms.

The most usual manner of addressing persons of this position is to write in the third person. A note of this kind, couched in courteous language, cannot give offence. *A faithful servant* being entitled not alone to our confidence, but to our esteem, may be addressed as 'Dear ——.'

The nicest people do not deem it derogatory to their rank to adopt this form of address. *Inferiors* should address their superiors as '*Madam*,' or at most as '*Dear Madam;*' not as 'My dear Friend,' or ' My dear Mrs. ——.'

CHAPTER II.

FURTHER HINTS FOR THE VARIOUS KINDS OF LETTERS.

I. FAREWELL LETTERS.

A farewell letter is that which we write to take leave of one with or near whom we have lived, and from whom we are about to be separated for a shorter or longer time.

The special characteristics of letters of this class are affection and regret.

In these two words everything is contained; therefore they should be the pervading sentiments of our letter, if the farewell is only for a short

time, such as that taken after a month's visit,
annually renewed, or a few days' hospitality kindly
shown us, our letter may be sprightly and playful.[1]
But if the absence is to be for long, above all if it is
likely to be for ever, then our pen should, as it
were, be steeped in tears.

And how can we write otherwise? How many
clouds, looming in the distance, shadow with deepest
sadness the parting hour! Trials, sickness, death,
spectre-like, arise before us till instinctively we ask
ourselves, Shall the voice so loved ever again fall
upon our ear; the eye so gentle ever meet our gaze;
the warm hand-clasp greet us as of yore?

The general ideas for a farewell letter are:

1. The pain at parting, together with the earnest
hope that we shall one day meet again.

2. A touching allusion to all the associations of
the past—the pleasures enjoyed, the friends known,
the sorrows shared, the studies pursued, the works
begun and perhaps left unfinished, the scenes so
often visited together.

> "They are remembered as a flower
>   Of richest tint, its bloom gone by;
> Or as the string of sweetest power,
>   That, broken, wakes the minstrel's sigh;
> As rainbow of a bright, fresh morn,
>   That storms have scattered and o'ercast—
> As all that to a heart, outworn,
>   Is saddening as the beauteous past."

---

[1] It would be a great breach of politeness to neglect to
write to thank a host or hostess, of whom one has been the
guest even for a few days.

3. A minute enumeration of the *souvenirs* we take with us—*souvenirs* enhanced a thousand times in value by the associations connected with them. A flower plucked, a picture received, a book read together, a drawing executed, a poem composed; things trifling in themselves—yet priceless in our eyes from the memories entwined around them.

4. Those Christian thoughts so fraught with consolation under every circumstance—the prayers offered at the same shrine, the union of spirit *there*.

5. The promise of an interchange of letters. For who does not yearn for tidings of the absent friend, and feel the truth of these words ?—

" We part, but carry on our way
    Some loved one's plaintive spirit-tune ;
That, as we wander, seems to say—
    Affection lives on faith—' Write soon !' "

6th, and last. The sweet reunion, at least in heaven.

"Look up ! look up ! should be the cry,
    'Mid darkness, doubt, and woe ;
We see a Life-star in the sky
    That does not shine below."

The special difficulties of farewell letters :

To those who are united to each other by the ties of friendship or esteem, letters of this kind can present no difficulties.

As to those who merely write through etiquette, by modifying the ideas found in those hackneyed forms, so aptly styled '*saddles for every horse,*' they may perhaps be able to fill up a page or two.

II. LETTERS FOR FESTIVE OCCASIONS.

To this class belong the letters which affection prompts us to write to our relatives, friends and superiors on the recurrence of the different anniversaries of note, such as that of a birthday, Christmas-tide, the New Year, etc.

Everyone is gratified at being remembered on those occasions :

> "The old man may smile while he listens, and feel
> He hath little time longer to stay ;
> Still he liketh to hear from the lips that are dear,
> 'Many happy returns of the day !'"

The special characteristics of such letters are *affection* for our friends, *respect* for those to whom we write through courtesy—affection which shows itself in quite a special way on those occasions by inviting to its aid all the resources of the intellect. In writing to those dear to us we may chat freely on every subject, reiterating the expression of our good wishes, our affection, our gratitude, etc.

In our congratulatory letters to superiors, while keeping in mind the respect due to them, our style may be less reserved than usual.

General ideas for letters of this class :

Written merely through etiquette, the above are

exceedingly difficult, and perhaps instead of a letter it would be better to send our card.

But at all events we must not forget that letters of this kind cannot be too short, and that where one phrase would suffice it would be superfluous to write four.

Children writing to their parents should express:

1st. The pleasure they feel in offering their congratulations.

2nd. The good wishes they entertain for them— and here what is it that affection will not suggest? Under the spell of the moment, these wishes will glow with an intensity which only the heart can give. A child will speak of the joys he or she hopes may surround the loved ones of the home circle, of sorrows spared, of afflictions lightened, etc.

3rd. Such a letter might conclude, in the ingenuous language of childhood, with the expression of plans for the happiness of the loved parents to whom so much is due.

The letter of a *protégé* should speak of his gratitude—his good fortune in possessing so kind and devoted a friend as his benefactor—a friend of whom he hopes always to prove himself worthy, and the memory of whose goodness shall be indelibly engraved on his heart.

The favours received from him might be enumerated in detail. Finally, he could express a hope that so precious a life may long be spared.

The subjects for festive occasions are most

5

copious, for it rarely happens that either the occasion itself or the flowers or other present that usually accompanies the letter fails to suggest some happy idea that may serve as the plea for a delicate compliment. A picture, a flower, an embroidered purse, a piece of furniture, a book of poems, a musical album, a new work, a contribution towards a journal, each may bear a graceful allusion to the tastes of its recipient.

Religious sentiments are too often excluded from such letters. Our letter should not be, it is true, a sermon. But is not God the author of all we have and are? What therefore is more natural than that He should be, as it were, interwoven with our good wishes for our friends?

LINES SENT WITH AN ALBUM.

Father revered, accept our gift ;
　　E'en simple though it be,
Fain would thy children hope 'twill prove
　　Not valueless to thee.

For it shall reassemble friends,
　　The cold world scattered o'er ;
Shall give them back unchanged in aught,
　　E'en as in days of yore.

And when Death's icy hand hath smote
　　Some cherished one and kind,
Intact beneath our album's care
　　The features loved thou'lt find.

The smile that lighted at thy voice,
　　The friendship-beaming eye,
Shall greet thee still, still on thee rest,
　　As in bright years gone by.

III. Condolence Letters.

Letters of this class are such as are written to those in affliction, to sympathize with them. The great object of them is to endeavour to sustain the sorrowing in the hour of trial.

The occasions on which letters of this kind may be written are as manifold as the sufferings to which humanity is heir.

Now it is a loved one that has been snatched away by death, and the wound is deep in proportion to the loss sustained, the suddenness of the event, or the sufferings incident to it.[1] Now it is a trial of a pecuniary nature that has prostrated hopes the highest, bringing adversity and a host of other misfortunes in its train.

Or it may be the forced or voluntary departure of some loved friend, whose absence has left a void which sympathy strives to fill.

Again, it may be the misconduct of a child that rends his mother's heart.[2]

In these and a thousand similar circumstances, letters of condolence are expected from us.

---

[1] Good taste suggests that we write on mourning paper to those with whom we would sympathize on the occasion of a death.

[2] There are trials which even the tenderest hand may not touch. Nothing but the intimation of them from the person concerned could authorise our alluding to them.

The characteristics of letters of this kind are :

1. Eagerness to console ; friendship is never tardy.

2. Affection, which manifests itself by its sympathy and devotedness. Never does the poor heart need the support of affection more than when the hand of sorrow is pressing on it.

3. A religious spirit, which alone is capable of offering true and solid consolation, based as it is on hopes that never can deceive.

The general ideas that should form the substance of a letter of condolence are :

1. To express the deep regret we ourselves feel.

2. To expatiate at length on the severity of the trial of the person we would console ; but great tact is necessary in recalling the cause of the suffering. On this subject no precise rules can be laid down without a knowledge of the disposition of the individual to whom we write. Such a one likes to hear the object of his grief spoken of. Such another shrinks from all that could recall the memory of it. The words of the poet but too well testify this :

> " Oh, never breathe a lost one's name,
>   To those who called that one their own ;
> It only stirs the smouldering flame
>   That burns upon a charnel-stone.
> The heart will ache and well-nigh break,
>   To miss that one for ever fled ;
> And lips of mercy should not wake
>   A love that cherishes the dead."

3. To try gradually to raise the thoughts to the great Soother and Sanctifier of sorrows.

There are some trials that can be alleviated only inasmuch as the words of comfort have been, as it were, suggested by the Crucifix.

4. If there is question of a pecuniary loss, we should point out the way of repairing it, should that be feasible; but our great aim should be to whisper hope, and thus reanimate the drooping spirit by kind and consoling words.

Faults to be avoided in letters of condolence:

In letters of this kind *long* and *trite* reflections must be carefully avoided. Common-place consolations jar on the feelings of those in deep affliction. The soul in sorrow is exclusively occupied with her own sad thoughts, and cannot understand that our attention should be diverted from these; we must therefore *particularize,* and strive to suit our words to such a one and such a sorrow.

2. *Lectures* and *advice* in letters of condolence would be misplaced. In the first deep anguish of bereavement, advice seems almost a mockery. The poor suffering heart, unable to appreciate, almost repels it.

> " I pray thee cease thy counsel,
> Which falls into my ear as profitless
> As water in a sieve : give not me counsel,
> Nor let no comforter delight mine ear
> But such a one whose wrongs do suit with mine."

To advise superiors would argue an ignorance of the rules of good-breeding, which regard such a proceeding as presumption ; to advise inferiors might seem to savour of reproach. We must wait till the first deep anguish has subsided, and the 'bruisèd heart' is somewhat healed, before we venture to offer our advice.

IV. LETTERS OF ADVICE.

The letters of admonition written by parents to their children, superiors to their inferiors, a friend to his friend, may be classed under this heading.

Even in cases where an advice is likely to be ill received, it must be written under pain of incurring a serious responsibility when there is question of preventing a fault, leading one back to the path of duty, or inculcating the performance of some important action.

But outside of these circumstances, in which an advice is *strictly obligatory*, there are countless others in which it may be given profitably. A child, for instance, leaves the parental roof, and a parent, brother, or sister may trace out a line of conduct to be pursued by him.

Again, a friend placed in an embarrassing position consults us as to how *we* should act under similar circumstances.

Or, a book, a poem, has been or is about to be published, and the author asks our opinion of it, etc.

The general characteristics of letters of advice are good sense, tact, and affection.

Good sense is necessary, because all advice should be guided by wisdom and experience.

When we speak conscientiously and prudently, even though the person addressed may be annoyed for the moment, still when the first impulse of anger has subsided, he will perceive his error and own that our *advice was right.* Tact is requisite, to prevent our wounding the feelings and awakening the pride of the person we advise. A short, blunt manner would be sure to produce these effects, and thus prevent any beneficial results from our letter. It is tact that teaches one to avoid all assumption of authority, as well as every appearance of pique in giving advice. It likewise inspires one to speak in terms the most insinuating, as, for instance :

' It seems to me that you might . . .' ' You, who are so clear-sighted, don't you think . . .' 'The course I advise is that which I would pursue myself, but is it really the right one ?' etc.

It is a recognised fact that the more gifted one is, the more unassuming he is both as to his manner of giving advice to those who consult him and the allowances he makes for their shortcomings.

The third essential of a letter of advice is affection, so as to leave no doubt that the advice is dictated by friendship and esteem, even though the words in which it is conveyed may be a little severe.

The general ideas that should form a letter of advice.

It is important to remember that these vary, first, according to the person that writes; secondly, according to the person written to; thirdly, and above all, according to the nature of the advice to be given.

A clergyman or parent may write more authoritatively than a friend.

The following, however, are general ideas for all letters of advice :

1st. The memory of the friendship and affection which once existed, or still exists, between us and the person to whom we write, which alone prompts us.

2nd. The happiness of directing, even though from a distance, a mind and heart for whose welfare we are so solicitous—or the pain we feel at no longer perceiving in one in whom we are deeply interested those sentiments which formerly were such a source of consolation to us.

3rd. The obligation we are under of using every effort to prevent the dear one from straying farther away from God.

4th. A moving appeal to the happy dispositions of bygone days.

5th. The firm hope that our letter will be listened to with the same docility as was our voice in days of yore.

The difficulties of letters of advice.

These proceed from either of two causes :

1st. A want of authority. Few things irritate

more than an advice given unsolicited by one who has no right to give it. The conduct of the beggar, who haughtily replied, when told to work instead of begging, that it was money, not advice, he asked, is exemplified every day.

2nd. *A want of tact.* For instance, our opinion is asked about something which is already done, and we give it as freely as if the matter were still an open question. The course to be followed under the circumstance is either to approve or to keep silence.

As a rule, our advice should be given at the voice of entreaty only.

V. LETTERS OF SOLICITATION.

Under this title we class all letters written to ask favours.

Letters of this kind, when addressed to a sovereign or minister, are called *petitions*, or *memorials*.

All petitions should be written on *letter-paper*, and one page should be left blank, in order that the person addressed may write his remarks on it. There is a particular form to be observed in memorials, and this should be studied.

The characteristics of letters of solicitation are:

1st. Clearness and precision in the statement of the request.

2nd. Respect in the manner of stating it.

3rd. Force and perspicuity in the reasons given.

4th. Tact to awaken the interest of the person

addressed, and thus more easily obtain the favour asked.

The general ideas of which letters of this class should be composed are:

1st. To endeavour to enlist the goodwill of him to whom we write by reminding him of his well-known benevolence and love of justice, which is the theme of every tongue.

2nd. To dwell on the importance of the favour we ask—an importance so great that without it we must fail to . . . with it we might . . .

3rd. To speak of the applause with which the granting of this boon would be received on every side, of our undying gratitude, and that of our family.

- 4th. To show how easily it might be granted, owing to the position, influence, etc., of him of whom it is asked.

Difficulties of letters of solicitation.

The faults to be avoided in this class of letters are :

1st. Prolixity. Most persons, particularly those occupying high posts, have but little leisure, and the mere sight of a long letter prejudices them against us even before the perusal of it.

2nd. Pride and presumption. These two vices, odious in anyone, are intolerable in a supplicant.

3rd. Meanness. To ask is not to cringe. Though we must always be deferential, still we must also maintain a noble self-respect, and never descend to servility or flattery. Never should we either

promise or ask anything for which we would afterwards have cause to blush, as contrary to honour
or to duty.

*

*   *

ANSWERS TO REQUESTS.

The answers to all petitions may be summed up
in three words : *To grant, to refuse, to promise.*

1. To grant.— Assuredly there is no sweeter
privilege than to be able to comply with a request.   Happy a thousand times he who, without injury to conscience, can always do what he is
asked.

No learned research is needed to teach us how to
say ' *Yes* ' when we know well that this ' *Yes* ' will
give pleasure.   And yet, if it is true of a favour,
that ' *the manner in which it is given is a true gift
in itself,*' would it not be worth one's while to try
to acquire it ?   Still, this is a secret which affection and refinement alone can teach.

2. To refuse.—This must always be a painful
duty ; and all the resources of politeness and
language must be resorted to in order to avoid
incurring the resentment, if not the enmity, of the
person disobliged.   A dry ' *No*' sometimes inflicts
a deep wound.   Let us try to lessen the disappoint-
ment by saying how pained we feel at having to
write what it must be so painful to read—that we
have deferred replying with the hope of being able

to grant the favour—the efforts we made to this effect—our desire of being of service on a future occasion, etc.

3. To promise.—When there is a probability of our being able to grant the favour asked of us, we should *at once* write to say so. A tardy answer, even if given in the affirmative, is of comparatively little value in the eyes of those to whom it is addressed, from the seeming want of interest evinced by the delay. Let us never be chary of kind cheering words. The bright inspiriting tone is infectious, and infuses its genial influence even into the most despondent, for—

> "What is hope ?—the beauteous sun
> Which colours all it shines upon ;
> The beacon of life's dreary sea—
> The star of immortality !"

VI. Letters of Excuse.

These are letters which are written to clear ourselves from an unjust imputation, or to apologize should we be really in fault.

We shall allude here only to light faults. Unfortunately, were it not for the veil with which affection and friendship hide our shortcomings, scarce a day would pass on which we would not have to appeal to the indulgence of others for our want of thoughtfulness and consideration in their regard.

*Candour, and self-control, are the characteristics
of letters of this description.*

Candour, by which we own and express a desire to
repair our fault if we have really been in error.

Self-control, aided by which we establish our
innocence with calmness and dignity, should we
have been wronged. At its dictates we will
refrain from all asperity of language, and from
directly accusing another unless really compelled
to do so.

The general ideas for a letter of excuse are :
If we are guilty.

1. A humble avowal of our fault, together with
the expression of our desire to atone for it.

2. To endeavour to extenuate it—ascribing it to
temper, the impulse of the moment, the circumstances in which we were placed ; in a word, to try
to show that it did not proceed from malice.

3. To promise a change of conduct.

4. To offer to make any satisfaction that may be
demanded of us, even though it involve much personal sacrifice.

5. To thank in anticipation for the pardon
which, from the well-known generosity of the
person offended, we feel will be granted.

If innocent.

1. To say simply that we are not in fault, and
endeavour to prove it.

2. To appeal to the justice and impartiality of
him to whom we write.

3. Never to insinuate that the accusation has been instigated by malice, at least unless we have very positive proofs that such is the case. We should merely say that our accuser has been misinformed, and bring forward testimonies to prove it.

4. To say how deeply we prize the esteem of him with whom we seek to exonerate ourselves.

5. To apologize should any hasty word have escaped us.

The special difficulties of a letter of excuse :

These proceed from the *warmth* with which we are wont to defend ourselves. We accuse, exaggerate, and multiply complaints and recriminations. Much calmness and self-possession are, as we have already remarked, necessary in letters of this kind. We should speak *firmly*, without doubt, but we should always speak politely. However aggrieved we may be, a courteous disavowal of the fault avails us far more than an angry one.

VII. LETTERS OF CONGRATULATION.

A letter of congratulation is one that is written to those we love or esteem, or in whom we are interested, to express the pleasure we feel at any good fortune they may have experienced. Thus we write to a brother, relative, or family friend, to offer our congratulations on the success achieved in a literary undertaking, an examination brilliantly passed, a situation obtained, a restoration to health, an auspicious event of any kind that has occurred in the family, etc. We also congratulate our benefactors and superiors in case of their receiving any promotion or honourable distinction, etc.

The general ideas for a letter of this class.

If we really love those to whom we write, the heart will speak spontaneously, inspiring not merely the sentiments but even the very words in which to give them utterance. If we are only impelled to write by politeness, and our letter must be a complimentary one, the following ideas could be worked out.

1. To express our pleasure at the fortunate event that has occurred, or the favour that has been obtained.

2. To say that this favour was anticipated as but a just reward.

3. To felicitate him who has received the favour, but to congratulate still more him who by conferring it has given so sure a proof of his discernment.

4. To expatiate on the advantages of the compliment received, or the joy which the news of it diffused on every side, and on the good which such a favour will effect, etc.

The special difficulties of letters of this kind.

The composition of congratulatory letters is generally attended with difficulty. As it is by no means easy to invest them with the charm of freshness or novelty, they are liable to become dull and insipid.

1. Difficult, because the compliment, if too delicate, is likely to be misunderstood.

2. If exaggerated, it may possibly annoy.

3. If it is a little cold, our formality may be attributed to jealousy.

4. If the compliment is too short, it displeases. If too long, it tires.[1]

A somewhat of vagueness in a compliment is not out of place. So blinded are we by self-love, that the more vague it is, the more flattering truths we discern in it. Would that the necessity for writing *formal* compliments did not exist! Happy are we when we are only called upon to congratulate those we love; then the compliment gushes forth from the heart fresh, joyous, delicate. It flatters without awakening a blush, pleases without wounding humility, and intensifies the affection that already exists.

VIII. LETTERS OF RECOMMENDATION.

Under this heading are included the letters by which we claim, in favour of another, the patronage with which a person of rank honours us, or the kindness which a friend has always expressed for us.

---

[1] It is related that when Louis XIV. had appointed M. de La Rochefoucauld to an important post, his Majesty wrote him a complimentary letter, on which he thought fit to consult the President, Rose. The letter was as follows : " *I rejoice with you, as your friend, on the favour I have just conferred on you as your master.*" " Sire," replied Rose, " since your Majesty deigns to do me the honour of consulting me, I will take the liberty of telling you that it is too sparkling and witty for a letter from a king to one of his subjects. The character of a sovereign requires more gravity." Louis, who was the politest man of the age, approved of the remark, and changed the letter.

The special characteristics of *letters of recommendation* are prudence and tact.

1. Prudence, to prevent our recommending those who are undeserving of confidence. We should incur the risk of seriously injuring another, or of encouraging unworthiness, incapacity, or sloth, were we to act inconsiderately, or through mere complacency or impulse in this matter.

2. Tact, to avoid hurting the feelings of those whom we recommend only through civility, and, as it were, reluctantly. A letter written under these circumstances must be very cautiously worded, so as not to offend him who has asked for the recommendation, nor yet deceive him to whom it is addressed.

The general ideas for a letter of recommendation vary according to the motives which inspire them. If it is charity that stimulates us to solicit pecuniary aid for one who is really destitute, or a situation for another in indigent circumstances who is competent to fill it, let us paint in strong colours the *necessities* of the one and *the qualifications* of the other. We should expatiate on the merit and happiness attached to good works, and the gratitude the person obliged will entertain for his benefactor.

If *friendship* is the mainspring of our letter, and that we write to a friend in favour of one who stands in the same relation to us, we should avail ourselves of the rights of friendship, urge the case warmly, speak of our personal gratitude, assume

6

the certainty of our request being granted, knowing as we do the worth of the persom for whom we plead, and the kindness of him to whom we apply.

If it is through mere courtesy we write, we should be very reserved and somewhat vague. Let us only praise him for whom we write on the points he deserves, and keep silence on all others. We should emphasize our unwillingness to influence in any way the decision of him to whom we are writing.

The special difficulties of letters of recommendation.

It is only in such letters as are written through condescension that any difficulties exist. When they originate in this motive great circumspection is necessary, for one neither wishes to compromise one's self nor yet disoblige nor deceive. They require much politeness and few words.

Custom requires that the letter of recommendation be given unsealed to the person in favour of whom it is written, and this renders the exercise of prudence still more imperative.

IX. LETTERS OF THANKS.

These, as the term implies, are letters written to express gratitude for a favour received.

Simple courtesy requires that we express our appreciation of any kindness conferred, and when unable to do so verbally we should not delay to express our thanks in writing. If our benefactor does not tire of lavishing favours, let us not tire of thanking him for them. The reputation of being grateful is invaluable to everyone. Perhaps we do not sufficiently know how to thank. Were there more gratitude in the world, the relations of man with his fellows would be much happier.

> "Sweet is the breath of vernal shower,
> The bee's collected treasure sweet,
> Sweet music's melting fall—but sweeter yet
> The still small voice of gratitude."

Let us not, therefore, hesitate to multiply letters of this description, nor should we confine our expressions of indebtedness to the *gift received*, but rather dwell on the kindness that prompted our friend to think of us. "It should be borne in mind that gifts are bestowed with a view to impart pleasure, therefore silence on this point would be an unpardonable omission—one that nothing save the most exceptionable circumstances could justify. Many a friendship, long, loyal, and self-sacrificing, rested at first on no stronger a foundation than a kind word. How often have we ourselves been made happy by kind words, in a manner and to an extent which we are quite unable to explain? No analysis enables us to detect the secret of their power."[1] Let us not, therefore, be sparing of them, particularly when there is a question of gratitude.

[1] Father Faber.

6—2

The special characteristic of letters of thanks is affection.

It is here especially that the heart should speak. If the intellect show itself it should only be in passing; by a word, perhaps, but nothing more. Too witty a letter might obtain for us the credit of being clever writers, but it would not go to prove that we were grateful.

The general ideas for letters of this kind are :

1. To testify the mingled sentiments of surprise, joy, admiration, and gratitude awakened by the sight of the gift, or the news of the favour granted us.

2. An unemphatic but graceful allusion to the importance of the favour, or the value or utility of the gift.

3. To say what we purpose to do with it, how carefully we intend to preserve it.

4. To express the gratification afforded us by this proof of remembrance from one whom we love or esteem so highly.

5. In fine, to assert in few, but expressive words, our deep and lasting gratitude.

The special difficulties of letters of thanks.

Perhaps some of the ill success of letters of this class proceeds from want of tact, which leads us to be egotistical and also to use exaggerated expressions in offering thanks for the favour received. Such as : *Never did friend carry kindness to the extent you have done. My whole life will be inadequate to repay it,* etc.

Another fault to be avoided—and this refers exclusively to the very young and unsophisticated —is that of regarding *gifts* as *loans*, and expressing an intention of making a return for them. Thus, very little children, on receiving a gift from a schoolfellow, will frequently write to say, ' I am very much obliged for your nice present, and I hope soon to send you one in return.'

But even very young children should be taught that this is not a polite thing to do. True, it is quite allowable to be kind to those who have been kind to us, and to compliment them when the occasion offers, but it would be very bad taste to allude to our intention of doing so.

A fourth and singularly ungraceful fault is that which sometimes leads persons, thoughtlessly without doubt, to depreciate the present made them, to say, for instance, ' I am very grateful for the book you so kindly sent me, *even though it is not the newest edition.*' Or, ' I am exceedingly obliged for the piece of work, but unfortunately it does not harmonise with the colours of either the carpet or curtains.'

And here it may not be out of place to remind our young friends that when we are offering a gift to another, it would be bad taste to say that *it is useless to us*, or that *we do not care for it.* To ask a person to accept a thing on which *we set no value*, would be but a poor compliment ; whereas in reality the more precious anything is, the more pleasure one feels in presenting it to a friend. But it is not to be understood from this that we are to extol our own gift.

X. LETTERS OF REPROOF.

These are letters that are written to another to point out his faults, whether deliberate or otherwise. Everyone is not entitled to write letters of this kind. To have the right to do so, one must have acquired a certain authority over the delinquent, either by benefits conferred, social position, very intimate friendship, or above all, duty.

The special characteristic of a letter of reproof is prudence, which waits *to be quite sure of a fault* before taxing a person with it. Prudence always supposes an error less than it seems, and abstains from harsh expressions, because it always bears in mind that "No one was ever corrected by a sarcasm; crushed perhaps, if the sarcasm was clever enough—but drawn nearer to God, never."[1] Prudence also avoids a line of conduct that would lead to the supposition of the reproof being actuated by revenge or malice. If it is against ourselves personally that the offence was committed, we should merely *glance* at the fault, extenuate its guilt, and write, not so much for the purpose of pointing it out, as for that of assuring the erring one of our forgiveness. If there is only question of a little want of deference, we may show by a playful word that we have forgotten it.

[1] Father Faber.

The general ideas for a letter of reproof.

If the faults are of a really serious nature which our duty obliges us to point out, and the delinquent is slow to realize the fact :—

1. We must represent in forcible terms how serious they are in themselves and as regards the person concerned; let us point out their probable consequences, the injury they may do to the reputation of the offender, the danger of their leading to a downward course.

2. Let us point out the means of repairing the past, and, if possible, offer to aid in the good work.

3. We should express an earnest hope that our advice will not be devoid of fruit, and dwell on the happiness which we, in common with all those who have been grieved by the faults in question, shall feel in seeing them atoned for.

4. Let us paint in vivid colours how honourable and praiseworthy it is to own and repair one's faults.

The special difficulties of letters of reproof.

The only difficulty of letters of this class arises from a *want of kindness. Kindness must never be excluded from a reproof.* It alone has the power of robbing painful truths of their bitterness. It heals where harsh words irritate; "kindness rouses the long-dormant self-respect, with which grace will speedily ally itself, and purify it by the alliance. It causes the first actions of the recovering soul to be actions on high principles and from generous motives. It shields moral convalescence from the dangers that beset it."[1]

Unfortunately, it sometimes happens that when faults are serious, and of frequent occurrence, we lose all hope of the amendment of the offender; and yet

"Something of good may still be there,
  Though its voice may never be heard aloud ;
For, while black with the vapours of pestilent air,
  There's a silver lining to every cloud."

XI. NOTES OF INVITATION.

These notes, as the title implies, are such as are written to invite persons to an entertainment, or ceremony.

The special characteristics of these are *simplicity* and *elegance.*

All superfluous words must be omitted, and though the forms vary sometimes, still the changes that occur in them are very slight.

In the Appendix will be found some models of the style of invitations used in good society, and which may be copied literally. Formerly invitations were written on note-paper. That is now tabooed, and invitations for all ceremonious occasions are printed on cards, models of which are given. Happily this spares much trouble, as the lady of the house has merely to fill up the blanks on such cards. It ought hardly to be necessary to set off the corner with the letters R.S.V.P. (*Répondez*

---

[1] Father Faber.

s'il vous plait), as it is to be hoped that few would be so thoughtless, not to say so deficient, in politeness, as to leave an invitation unnoticed.

With regard to the less formal invitations, the examples given are not meant for literal imitation. Their only object is to show that one friend inviting another is not obliged to use any set form of words, and the simpler and more natural the note is the better.

XII. COMMERCIAL CORRESPONDENCE.

This comprises *circulars* announcing perhaps the erection of a house, the receipt of important articles, the change of ownership of a well-known establishment, etc., orders and commands, notices of agreements entered into, letters of exchange, receipts, etc.

1. In giving orders to commercial houses, we should specify the quality, quantity, and price of the articles we require, mention when expected, the mode of conveyance, etc., signifying whether to be prepaid or not.

2. When returning goods, to represent politely that they lack the qualities guaranteed. Finally, to request that the above be exchanged or a reduction made in the price.

APPENDIX.

LETTERS ON VARIOUS SUBJECTS.

FAREWELL LETTERS.

Kyber Pass Lodge, Wicklow,
3rd May, 18—.

MY DEAR ——,

On my return here this evening I was told by the servant that you had called to say good-bye, and had left a note. I cannot say how grieved I am that I should have been from home, and should have missed seeing you. I found some comfort in looking at the photograph you have left on my table. You had gone, but left your shadow. I send you now my photograph; truly a sad exchange at parting—shadow for shadow! the shadows, as it seems to me, cast by the light of happy days we spent together; for our bright hours *do* cast shadows as they leave us—yet am I right? Does not *photograph* mean, drawn in light? My rusty Greek suggests that derivation. Yours shall be a picture drawn by light, *in* light; a gleam, and not a shadow in my book of shadows. How I should love the sun for casting such a gleam as to recall for ever—at least for my little 'ever'—the features of my friend!

Written also in light in my memory are the days

you and I have spent together—days of work and days of play, bright days all. I do not dare to hope for days as bright again. Ours was certainly a friendship of work: we shared the labours as we shared the success. Both are past now, and with my parting from you I seem to see my parting also from the energy with which your co-operation and example filled me, and from the success which your talents always ensured, and which it was my good fortune to share. I cannot bear to think of how much of my life ends with your visit and this letter. It is a deep comfort that I can look back on the years we spent together, and see there nothing that ever came between us, not even a word—I fancy not even a thought in which we were not true to each other. May our truth be lasting—truth always is. I used to sing to you, 'True till Death;' when I have spirits to open my piano I will sing that song again—the farewell song to many songs. For once the post-hour is merciful in making me break off a letter which would continue only to express more fully and more painfully the genuine sorrow of

Your ever devoted friend,

————.

Lord Macaulay to Lord Lansdowne.

Gravesend, February 15, 1834.

DEAR LORD LANSDOWNE,

I had hoped that it would have been in my power to shake hands with you once more before my departure . . .

I cannot leave England without sending a few lines to you; and yet they are needless. It is unnecessary for me to say with what feelings I shall always remember our connection, and with what interest I shall always learn tidings of you and of your family.

Yours most sincerely,

T. B. MACAULAY.

LETTERS OF CONGRATULATION.

Fern Vale, May 2, 18—.

MY DEAR ——,

You are so secluded these times that one cannot have the pleasure of giving you a *vivâ voce* greeting. Allow me to offer you through this paper messenger a very happy feast, and a long train of anniversaries.

Sincerely yours,

——.

The Royal Marine Hotel, Kingston,
December 31, 18—.

MY DEAR ——,

As I know that you will think of me
to-morrow, and that I shall not be forgotten in
your prayers, I cannot refrain from telling you that
you shall not be forgotten either in my prayers
or in my best wishes for your present and future
happiness.

The joy-bells will welcome 18— to-night. Though
their tones will soon be lost in the world amidst
its confusion and discord, I hope that they will be
echoed on through all the months in your peaceful,
happy home, and that they won't have quite died
out this day twelvemonths in the tranquil halls
of ——.

I trust that you will have your share of peace
and joy, and that past trials will be forgotten in
future happiness.

I remain, my dear ——,
Yours very sincerely,

_____

ANSWER TO A LETTER OF CONGRATULATION.

Dublin, Christmas Eve, 18—.

MY DEAR ——,

Need I say how sincerely I reciprocate the
kind wishes every line of your note breathes ?

A 'happy Christmas' I pray our new-born
Saviour to grant you and yours, and to turn the

cloud which for a while has been overshadowing
you into sunshine. How can I thank you for your
Christmas gifts ?

Only believe me to be, as ever,

Yours truly,

———.

CONDOLENCE LETTER ON THE DEATH OF A WIFE.

Mount St. Lawrence, May 4th, 18—.

MY DEAR———,

I know all. It was the first thing I saw in
this morning's paper, and I would see no more.
Now that I am calm, I send you this sad, sad line.
Where and when am I to pay my last duty of affection to her whom we have lost ? Her death, God
knows, is grief enough to me. But knowing as I
do what her life was—how good, how sad—I could
bear the thought of her going to better things. But
what I cannot bear, is the thought that you are
alone in such a sorrow. Such bereavements make
a solitude round the heart into which no human
comforter may enter. God alone, who has sent the
sorrow, can console it; and I pray that He may stay
you up until, the violence of your grief having subsided, you may be able to recognise His hand in this
trial, His love in its pressure on your poor heart.

I cannot write—you know why. Words may be
fitting later on. Now, silence is better, and prayer.
Oh, do not forget to pray. Hold His hand fast;

until your own hour comes, you will never have more need of His loving support than in this hour of your bitterest affliction.

A telegram will be sufficient to let me know what I am to do.

God help you, my poor fellow.   Those words have meaning *now*.

In deep grief, and with fullest sympathy,

I remain,

Yours affectionately,

———.

LETTER OF ADVICE.

Merrion Square, Dublin,
April 14, 18—.

MY DEAR ———,

I have indeed to apologize very much for not having at once replied to your note of Wednesday. The sole cause of the delay has been my anxiety to answer with perfect accuracy the inquiry which you paid me the compliment of proposing to me.

Putting together the feminine personification to which classical ideas have subjected the seasons, and the circumstance to which you refer of Thomson describing some of them (winter, I suppose) under a masculine personification, I thought I would adduce a conflict of authorities to clear up the controversy.   I have, therefore, looked up and down among some of the poets for evidence on which to conclude as to their mode of solving the problem ;

and, before I draw any inference, I shall lay a few details of the evidence before you.

Thomson himself says :

> ' 'Tis done ! dread winter spreads *its* latest glooms
> And reigns tremendous o'er the conquered year.'

Spenser, in a description of winter, says :

> ' Lastly came Winter, clothèd all in frieze,
> Chattering *his* teeth for cold that did him chill.'

Keats, in 'An Address to Autumn,' treats it under a *masculine* personification, and Mrs. Hemans writes :

> ' Now Autumn strews on every plain
> *His* mellow fruit and fertile grain.'

And Sir W. Scott' :

> ' Autumn departs, but still *his* mantle's fold
> Rests on the groves of noble Somerville,' etc.

But John Clare :

> ' A solitaire through Autumn's wan decay,
> He heard the toothing robin sound *her* knell."

Spenser says of ' Summer ':

> ' In *his* hand he bore
> A bowe and shafts, as he in forest green
> Had hunted late,' etc.

Spenser also makes 'Spring' *masculine*, whereas from many other poets it receives a *feminine* personification.

The year is masculine in McCarthy's ' Bridal of the Year.'

It is feminine in Shelley, where he says :

> ' And the year,
> On the earth *her* death-bed, in a shroud of leaves, dead is
> lying.'

Now, what I infer from this pedantic collection
of quotations is, that it is entirely a matter of taste
and convenience, both in poetry and in the drama,
as to whether the personification be masculine or
feminine.   There are numerous authorities for both
modes of treatment, so whatever course be followed,
it will not be amenable to criticism.   It would even
seem to be quite free to vary the personification as
one pleases, the details depending altogether on the
aspect under which the season is portrayed.   If
the winter be represented as wild and turbulent,
and committing all sorts of havoc, no doubt he
should be depicted as one of the boisterous and less
gentle sex ; but if it be dealt with as by Southey :

> ' And pleasant to the sobered soul,
> The silence of the wintry scene,
> When Nature shrouds herself entranced
> In deep tranquillity,'

there would be nothing inappropriate in the feminine personification.

I am sure you did not intend to get yourself
bored by such a dissertation as the present one,
when you put the question about the seasons to
me ; but one who is *professionally devoted* to
hunting up all critical inquiries generally perpe-
trates a regular sermon when appealed to on such

7

occasions. I cannot hope to impart to the result, the same pleasure I felt in following up the brief investigation.

Excuse such a long document.

My dear ——,

Yours very sincerely,

——.

LETTERS OF REPROOF.

To Lord Macaulay from his Father.

London, March 4, 1814.

MY DEAR TOM,

In taking up my pen this morning, a passage in Cowper almost involuntarily occurred to me. You will find it at length in his 'Conversations.'

> " Ye powers who rule the tongue, if such there are,
> And make colloquial happiness your care,
> Preserve me from the thing I dread and hate—
> A duel in the form of a debate.
> Vociferated logic kills me quite—
> A noisy man is always right."

You know how much such a quotation as this would fall in with my notions, averse as I am to loud and noisy tones, and self-confident, overwhelming, and yet, perhaps, very unsound arguments. And you will remember how anxiously I dwelt upon this point while you were at home. I have been in hopes that this half-year would witness a great change in you in this respect. My hopes, however, have been a little damped by something which I heard last week through a friend, who seemed to have received an impression that you had gained a high distinction among the young gentlemen at Shelford, by the loudness and vehemence of your tones. Now, my dear Tom, you cannot doubt that this gives me pain; and it does so not so much on account of the thing itself, as because I consider it a pretty infallible test of the mind within. I do long and pray most earnestly that the ornament of a meek and quiet spirit may be substituted for vehemence and self-confidence, and that you may be as much distinguished for the former as you have ever been for the latter. It is a school in which I am not anxious that any child of mine should take a high degree. If the people of Shelford be as bad as you represent them in your letters, what are they but an epitome of the world at large? Are they ungrateful to you for your kindnesses? Are they foolish and wicked and wayward in the use of their faculties? What is all this, but what we ourselves are guilty of every day? Consider how much in our case the guilt of such conduct is aggravated by our superior knowledge. We shall not have ignorance to plead in its extenuation as many of the people of Shelford may have. . . .

I am ever your most affectionate father,
ZACHARY MACAULAY.

7—2

LETTER OF EXCUSE.
From Lord Macaulay to his Father.

MY DEAR FATHER,

My mother's letter, which has just arrived, has given me much concern. The letter which has, I am sorry to learn, given you and her uneasiness, was written rapidly and thoughtlessly enough, but can scarcely, I think, as far as I remember its tenor, justify some of the extraordinary inferences which it has occasioned. . . I will, however, say this in my defence. Whatever the affectionate alarm of my dear mother may lead her to apprehend, I am not one of the 'sons of anarchy and confusion' with whom she classes me. I may be wrong as to the facts of what occurred at Manchester; but, if they be what I have seen them stated, I can never repent speaking of them with indignation. When I cease to feel the injuries of others warmly, to detest wanton cruelty, and to feel my soul rise against oppression, I shall think myself unworthy to be your son. . . . Were the elevation of a Cromwell, or the renown of a Hampden, the certain reward of my standing forth in the democratic cause, I would rather have my lips sealed on the subject than give my mother or you one hour of uneasiness. There are not so many people in the world that love me that I can afford to pain them for any object of ambition which it contains. If this assurance be not sufficient, clothe it in what language you please, and believe me to express myself in those words which you think the strongest and most solemn.

Affectionate love to my mother and sisters,

Farewell,

T. B. M.

LETTER OF CONGRATULATION ON A RETURN FROM THE CONTINENT.

Arabi Villas, April 12, 18—.

MY DEAR ——,

To think that anything under the heading 'Fashionable Intelligence' should have the power of putting me in the state of flutter and jubilation that I have been in for the last ten minutes! How *did* you get into the papers? For once I rejoice that the 'Queen walked out yesterday, that Lady Fitz-noodle had the honour, etc., that the Right Honourable Blatherum Bombast is getting over his gout;' for, attracted by this laughable list of absurdities, my eye wandered down till it came to news that made me clap my hands with delight, the news that your dear self 'has returned home after a prolonged absence in the South of France.' Indeed, the reporter (how I admire his inquisitive art, for I don't suspect you!) is right in saying 'prolonged,' till my hopes grew faint, and I thought your absence was to be for ever: an absence that I never could grow used to—a blank that was not only filled by no one, but was made even more conspicuous as every fresh figure appeared on the scene. For I have been thinking of you in everything—how you would have enjoyed some persons and things with me, and how gone with me in my dislike of others. Oh, no! not persons, only *things*. Not even our well-kept resolution of being total abstainers from gossiping letters could prevent me from fancying I was telling you every adventure, every joke, every little excitement. Now I shall rehearse them all so as to be ready for our first long chat. Won't it be a long one! Our reporter friend would say a 'prolonged interview.' I half expect we shall have to draw lots to decide who is to begin, else your French, and my English, both at high pressure and going on at the same time, would possibly result in some confusion. Where? When? And mind, none of your 'pressing engagements' is to shorten our *causerie*.

I am delighted you are having such a smiling welcome from our much-abused weather. Is it not better than the monotonously mild French stuff after all, that never would give one the welcome of this spring morning ?—a welcome in which I most heartily and joyfully join.

Till we meet, yours, as ever,

LETTERS OF THANKS.

Dublin, May 12, 18—.

MY DEAR MRS. ——,

Just one line to say that the beautiful book arrived quite safe. I need scarcely say that it will remind me of all in ——; though indeed it was not necessary for that purpose, as I can never forget the many acts of kindness I have received from you and yours. I hope you all continue well.

Please give my kind regards to everyone in ——.

Believe me,

Yours most faithfully,

——.

The Shelbourne Hotel, Dublin,

Jan. 7, 18—.

MY DEAR MRS. ——,

I cannot go to bed to-night without writing one word to express to you my sense of your extreme kindness to me to-day. I assure you that no incident in this or any other election for the county has given me such unmixed pleasure as the accident which brought me to your hospitable home.

Will you kindly always bear in mind that none of those who are bound to you by ties of gratitude and affectionate respect can exceed me in depth of sincere feeling.

Most gratefully and respectfully yours,

——.

Seafield, Jan. 18, 18—.

MY DEAREST ——,

With your unfailing friendship you have written to inquire how I am. I am (D.G.) very well. I have been, and am still, suffering from nervousness, which is often more distressing than actual illness, but otherwise I am very well.

It pains me very much that you should suffer uneasiness. The only reason of apathy or apparent forgetfulness on my part is the nervousness of which I complain, and the exhaustion which accompanies it.

I will, *as soon as possible*, see you.

Ever, my dear ——,

Yours most affectionately,

——.

Lord Macaulay to Lord Lansdowne.

London, Dec. 5, 1833.

DEAR LORD LANSDOWNE,

I delayed returning an answer to your kind letter till this day, in order that I might be able to send you some definite intelligence. . . . And now, dear Lord Lansdowne, let me thank you most warmly for the kind feeling which has dictated your letter. That letter is, indeed, but a very small part of what I ought to thank you for. That at an early age I have gained some credit in public

life; that I have done some little service to one
good cause; that I now have it in my power to
repair the ruined fortunes of my family, and to
save those who are dearest to me from the misery
and humiliation of dependence; that I am almost
certain, if I live, of obtaining a competence by
honourable means before I am past the full vigour
of manhood—all this I owe to your kindness. I
will say no more. I will only entreat you to
believe that neither now, nor on any former occasion, have I ever said one thousandth part of what
I feel. . . .

Believe me, ever,
Yours most faithfully and affectionately,
T. B. MACAULAY.

FRIENDLY LETTERS ON VARIOUS SUBJECTS.

Lord Macaulay to his Mother.

Trin. Coll., March 25, 1821.

MY DEAR MOTHER,

I entreat you to entertain no apprehension
about my health. My fever, cough and sore throat
have all disappeared for the last four days. Many
thanks for your intelligence about poor dear John's
recovery, which has much exhilarated me. Yet I
do not know whether illness to him is not rather
a prerogative than an evil. I am sure that it is

well worth while being ill to be nursed by a mother. There is nothing I remember with such pleasure as the time when you nursed me at Aspenden. The other night, when I lay on my sofa very ill and hypochondriac, I was thinking over that time. How sick and sleepless and weak I was, lying in bed, when I was told that you were come! How well I remember with what an ecstasy of joy I saw that face approaching me, in the middle of people that did not care if I died that night, except for the trouble of burying me! The sound of your voice, the touch of your hand, are present to me now, and will be, I trust in God, to my last hour. The very thought of these things invigorated me the other day; and I almost blessed the sickness and low spirits which brought before me associated images of a tenderness and an affection which, however imperfectly repaid, are deeply remembered. Such scenes and such recollections are the bright half of human nature and human destiny. All objects of ambition, all rewards of talent, sink into nothing compared with that affection which is independent of good or adverse circumstances, excepting that it is never so ardent, so delicate, or so tender as in the hour of languor or distress. But I must stop. I had no intention of pouring out on paper that which I am much more used to think than to express.

Farewell, my dear mother.

Ever yours affectionately,

T. B. MACAULAY.

Lord Macaulay to his Father, on the Death of his Sister.

Paris, Sept. 26, 18—.

MY DEAR FATHER,

This news has broken my heart. I am fit neither to go nor to stay. I can do nothing but sit in my room and think of poor dear Jane's kindness and affection. When I am calmer, I will let you know my intentions. There will be neither use nor pleasure in remaining here. My present purpose, as far as I can form one, is to set off in two or three days for England; and in the meantime to see nobody, if I can help it, but Dumont, who has been very kind to me. Love to all—all who are left me to love. We must love each other better.

T. B. M.

Lord Macaulay to his Father.

Calcutta, Oct. 12, 1836.

MY DEAR FATHER,

We were extremely gratified by receiving, a few days ago, a letter from you which, on the whole, gave a good account of your health and spirits. The day after to-morrow is the first anniversary of your little granddaughter's birthday. The occasion is to be celebrated with a sort of droll puppet-show, much in fashion with the natives— an exhibition much in the style of 'Punch' in England, but more dramatic and more showy . . .

. . . Within half a year after you read this, we shall be making preparations for our return. The feelings with which I look forward to that return, I cannot express. Perhaps I should be wise to continue here longer, in order to enjoy during a greater number of months the delusion—for I know it will prove a delusion—of this delightful hope. I feel as if I never could be unhappy in my own country—as if to exist on English ground and among English people, seeing the old familiar sights and hearing the sound of my mother tongue, would be enough for me. This cannot be; yet some days of intense happiness I shall surely have; and one of those will be the day when I again see my dear father and sisters.

Ever yours most affectionately,

T. B. MACAULAY.

From Lord Jeffrey to Macvey Napier, Esq.

May 2, 1837

MY DEAR N.,

What mortal could ever dream of cutting out the least particle of this precious work* to make it fit better into your *Review?* It would be worse than paring down the 'Pitt' diamond to fit the old setting of a dowager's ring. . . .

Still, I do not object whether it might not be best to serve up the rich repast in two courses; and on

---

* Macaulay's article on Bacon.

the whole I incline to that partition. A hundred and twenty pages might cloy even epicures, and would be sure to surfeit the vulgar ; and the biography and philosophy are so entirely distinct, and of not very unequal length, that the division would not look like a fracture.

FRANCIS JEFFREY.

From Sir Charles Gavan Duffy to the late J. F. Maguire.

Melbourne, April 22, 1863.

MY DEAR MAGUIRE,

Cashel Hoey, in a recent note (received by the last mail), mentions that you are engaged in a 'Life of Father Mathew,' and wish me to send you any correspondence in my possession. I *have* a number of letters from Father Mathew, but we are in the midst of a Session of Parliament, and I have not time to look for them, and scarcely time to scrawl this note. When I have a leisure hour I will find them and send them, or such of them as seem likely to be useful to you.

Many thanks for your friendly articles in the *Examiner* since I saw you last. You certainly do not forget your friends, though they may be at the other end of the earth.

Accept my hearty congratulations on your double triumph, civic and political. To be so often chief magistrate of one's native city is a rare and nearly unprecedented success.

Your Parliamentary labours I confess I cannot regard with the same pleasure. I am sure I would have died before this if *I* had continued to waste my life in asking justice from the British Parliament in vain. But you have been gifted with a more robust nature, and thrive in the hostile atmosphere.

Believe me,

My dear Maguire,

Very faithfully yours,

C. Gavan Duffy.

Letter of Introduction.

Dear ——,

The bearer of this note is one of the many who desire your acquaintance, and one of the few who deserve it.[1]

Yours truly,

Manzoni.

From —— to a Little Child.

The Hermitage, 11th Oct., 18—.

My Dear Child,

I am very glad to hear from you. You write just the sort of letter I like. You should see some people write letters ! They first go for a big dictionary, then they try to remember some big words, and, as these people never know how to spell, they

---

[1] Extracted from the *Dublin Review*, October, 1882.

look out for the big words in the big book, and then proceed to write a 'big letter.' You ask me to write you a 'big,' long letter. But I am sure you don't want a 'big' letter that neither you nor I can understand. These silly people—for they *are* silly, though they won't let you say it—when they want to have a letter particularly grand, go to a book where there are copies of letters that would do for one person just as well as for another (and that is not very well), and they copy out these fine letters just as you copy from your copy-book, only that they fill in the blank places, and put—very dishonestly as well as very foolishly—their *own* names in the blank places at the end. Well, Maudie, *we* are not likely to be as silly as that; and I am sure no one would ever mistake your nice little letter for one that was helped either by a dictionary or a letter copy-book.

Now I am not going to scold you for your spelling. I am not quite sure that I don't like your way in some cases better than the right way. For instance, 'tortise' is much plainer than 'tortoise,' which is the right way. However, as the word means crooked, I suppose the dictionary people (I wonder who *they* are?) thought the word should be spelt crookedly also. I am glad you told me about the tortoise. I had one when I was very small, and used to be puzzled, as you are, by the way it used to pull in its head to go to sleep. But then it must go to sleep almost as often and as easily as the fat boy in 'Pickwick.' But I forget; you haven't got that far yet.

When you are old and sensible, you will read such books. Old people want them to make them pleasant. You are always happy and pleasant, and need not go for your pleasure, any more than you go for your spelling, to books.

But about the tortoise. Wouldn't it be fun if *we* could pull in our heads like that? Imagine how nice it would be, just as our ears were going to be boxed, to pull in our heads, ears and all. I fancy we should be heard laughing inside, which would be much better than crying outside—wouldn't it? But I am afraid we would never do it, for we are too stiff-necked; and if we got our heads in, we might never be able to get them out again. Speaking of stiff-necks reminds me of your donkey. You say it is stubborn sometimes. I hope it is *only* it that is ever stubborn in your school. I have seen little girls trying, I suppose, to imitate the donkey by being stiff and stubborn, refusing to do what was wanted of them; and, like the donkey, they only got whipped all the more for being stupid. But, of course, they were much more stupid than the donkey, for they were naughty, which a donkey never is; for they know that it is not good or right to be stubborn and disobedient, and that it offends God, Who wishes us to do always readily and cheerfully what we are told to do.

And now, dear Maudie, I must say good-bye; for I have some serious work to do, much more serious than talking to you about tortoises and donkeys, though not half as pleasant. When you write again, tell me more about the tortoise; and this time you will spell it right. Also tell me, if you wish, whether *you* ever imitate that poor foolish donkey, or whether his example reminds you to be obedient and willing. For we can be taught even by a donkey !

I am ever, dear Maudie,

Your old friend,

EXTRACT FROM A LETTER OF LORD MACAULAY TO HIS NIECE.

MY DEAR LITTLE ALICE,

I quite forgot my promised letter, but I assure you that you were never out of my mind for three waking hours together. I have, indeed, had little to put you and yours out of my thoughts; for I have been living, these last ten days, like Robinson Crusoe in his desert island. I have had no friends near me, but my books and my flowers, and no enemies but those execrable dandelions. I thought that I was rid of the villains; but the day before yesterday, when I got up and looked out of my window, I could see five or six of their great, impudent, flaring yellow faces turned up at me. 'Only you wait, till I come down!' I said. How I grubbed them up ! How I enjoyed their destruction ! Is it Christian-like to hate a dandelion so savagely ? That is a curious question of casuistry.

8

ADDRESS

Presented to His Grace, the Most Rev. Dr. ——
Lord Archbishop of ——, on the occasion of a
Distribution of Prizes.

MY LORD ARCHBISHOP,

The gauzy veil that hides the breaking morn had scarce been drawn aside, the sleeping flowers, wooed by the sun's first rays, had only waked, when from every heart amongst us there issued a gladsome greeting to this auspicious day.

Your Grace's illustrious presence here conveys such honour, imparts such joy, as words fail to utter —reverentially, enthusiastically then, we bid you welcome—and present the homage of our deep devotedness. Gratitude, in whose golden depths lie hidden so many gems, would fain find vent in words; let then its voice be heard in music's swelling tide, in every note of silvery song, in the word and gesture of the personated native of sunny France, the Italian, or the dweller by the matchless Rhine. Swiftly seems it the golden hours have sped during the year just vanished, and the tedium and toil in pursuit of lore are now alike forgotten, as storms when the port is reached, and 'Heaven is all sunshine.' Hope whispers that in her sparkling fount there lies a pearl to crown pre-eminence. Ambition's banner has lured us on, and Glory's gilded plume has cast its spell around us. At the shrines of both

we have knelt that to-day our trophies might be
borne in triumph to your Grace's feet, be crowned
with the smile of your approbation.

And now, My Lord Archbishop, we would ask
your prized blessing, ere we leave these hallowed
walls. Fortified by it, we will go into the world
without, nor turn aside, though pleasure lure from
the holy precepts inculcated here. In soft persuasive accents they will whisper ever that the glory
of earth passes away, that its joys are fleeting as the
rose tints of morn, or the moon's dimpling smiles on
some fair lake—that woman's high aim must ever be
to school the heart for heaven, and shed around her the
odour of many virtues, that thus, this vanishing scene
ended, she may receive ' the fruit of her hands, and
her works praise her in the gates.' Accept, my
Lord Archbishop, some gems of nature, gathered by
affection's hand. These flowers ere long will fade and
die, but they will speak of others whose beauty,
whose fragrance, shall live for ever ; they bloom in
blissful Eden's bowers, they bask in her glorious
sunshine, they will yet dazzle, delight you there
through the long day of eternity.

Your Grace's grateful and devoted children,
THE PUPILS OF ——.

8—2

FORMAL INVITATIONS.

These, as we have already remarked, are printed cards. The following are some of the most usual forms :

AT HOME.

Lawn Tennis.   R.S.V.P.

AT HOME.

Dancing.   R.S.V.P.

Request the pleasure of

Company at Dinner.

R.S.V.P.

Request the pleasure of

Company at an Evening Party.

Dancing.　　　　　*R.S.V.P.*

Request the pleasure of

Company at a Garden Party.

R.S.V.P.

Request the pleasure of

Company on

On the occasion of the marriage of

R.S.V.P.

The same forms with the blanks filled up :

Mr. and Mrs. Osborne.

Mrs. Ellis.

AT HOME.

Monday, September 4th.

Lawn Tennis, 3 to 7.[1]   *R.S.V.P.*

Sybil Hill.

Mr., Mrs., and Miss Authistle.

Mrs. Lalor.

AT HOME.

Thursday, August 8th.

Dancing, 9 o'clock.   *R.S.V.P.*

Marble Hall.

[1] The hours may be varied according to the taste of the hostess, but those given here are generally observed in

Mr. and Mrs. Nugent .
Request the pleasure of
Captain, Mrs., and the Misses Norton's
Company at Dinner.
            Saturday, June 6th.

7.30 o'clock.   *R.S.V.P.*

Ashton Hall.

Mr. and Mrs. Ashlin
Request the pleasure of
    Sir John and Lady Burke's
Company at an Evening Party.
        Monday, July 4th.

Birchfield.
Dancing, 8 to 1.   *R.S.V.P.*

Captain and Mrs. St. Lawrence
Request the pleasure of
    Mr. and the Misses Lamb's
Company at a Garden Party.
        Wednesday, September 24th.

Richmond.
3 to 7.   *R.S.V.P.*

---

fashionable circles. The blanks, though filled up here to
illustrate what we mean, should never be printed, but always
written by the lady who issues the invitation.

Mr. and Mrs. St. George
Request the pleasure of
Mr. and Mrs. Southron's
Company, on Monday, Sept. 28,
At Gardiner's Street Church, 11 *o'clock.*
On the occasion of the marriage of their
daughter Linda ; and afterwards at breakfast
at Sorrell Lodge. R.S.V.P.

LESS FORMAL INVITATIONS.[1]

MY DEAR MRS. LALOR,

Will you, Mr. Lalor, and the girls favour us with your company at dinner on Tuesday, 11th inst., at seven o'clock ? Yours sincerely,

EDITH GREY.

Bushy Park, Saturday morning.

REPLY ACCEPTING.

MY DEAR MRS. GREY,

Mr. Lalor, the young people and myself, will with much pleasure accept your kind invtiation for Tuesday. Yours sincerely,

HILDA LALOR.

Sydney Terrace, Saturday.

REPLY DECLINING.

MY DEAR MRS. GREY,

We regret very much that we shall be unable to accept your kind invitation, as we have to leave town for a fortnight this evening.

HILDA LALOR.

---

[1] These of course are written on note-paper, and are never printed.

THE END.

ROBERT WASHBOURNE'S
CATALOGUE OF BOOKS,

18 PATERNOSTER ROW, LONDON.

Second Series of True Wayside Tales. By Lady Herbert. [*In the press.*

Our Esther. By M. F. S. Author of "Out in the Cold World." [*In the press.*

Life of Rev. Fr. Hermann (Discalced Carmelite). From the French of the abbé Charles Sylvain, by Mrs. F. Raymond-Barker. 8vo. cloth, 5s. 6d. ; stronger bound, 6s. 6d.

Links with the Absent ; or, Chapters on Correspondence. Arranged from various sources. By a Member of the Ursuline Community, Thurles, Translator of "Solid Virtue," &c. [*In the press.*

The Vatican and the Quirinal. Translated from the Italian, by Alexander Wood, M.A., F.S.A. 1s. 6d.

Works of St. Francis of Assisi. Translated by a Religious of the Order. 4s.

Treatise on the Way of Sorrows, followed by a Practical Method of Blessing, Erecting, and Solemnly Performing the Stations of the Way of the Cross. By F. Alexis Bulens, O.S.F., of the Monastery, West Gorton, Manchester. Cloth, 1s. 6d., red edges, 2s.

Killed at Sedan. A Novel. By Samuel Richardson, A.B., B.L., of the Middle Temple, author of "Noel d'Auvergne," &c. 10s. 6d.

Zeal in the Work of the Ministry. By Abbé Dubois. Translated. 10s.
"Everything in it breathes wisdom and prudence, and not less Christian faith, piety, and love."

Bobbie and Birdie ; or, Our Lady's Picture. A story for the very little ones. By Frances J. M. Kershaw. 2s. 6d.

Solid Virtue. By Father Bellécius, S.J. New edition, revised and corrected by a Religious of the Ursuline Community at Thurles. With a Preface by the Archbishop of Cashel and Emly. 7s. 6d.

Catholic Hymn Book. By Rev. Langton George Vere. 204 pages, price 2d. ; in cloth, 4d. This is the best and cheapest Hymn book printed. *An Abridged Edition is now ready.* Price 1d.

The Office of Holy Week, according to the Roman Rite. This edition gives (including the Ordinary of the Mass, and the Services generally included in Holy Week Books) the Vespers and Complin for every day of Holy Week ; the Blessing of the Holy Oils on Maundy Thursday ; and the Matins, Lauds, Mass, Vespers, and Complins of Easter Sunday. Price 1s.

..* *All other Books not mentioned in this Catalogue supplied.*

School Books, *with the usual reduction,* Copy Books, and other Stationery, Rosaries, Medals, Crucifixes, Scapulars, Incense, Candlesticks, Vases, &c., &c., supplied. FOREIGN BOOKS supplied. Catalogue containing very reduced prices, post free.

R. Washbourne, 18 Paternoster Row, London.

Agnes Wilmott's History and the Lessons it Taught. B
Mary Agatha Pennell, author of " Bertram Eldon " (1s.), " Nelli
Gordon " (6d.), &c. Fcap. 8vo., 1s. 6d. *[In the press*

For Better, Not for Worse. By Rev. Langton George Vere

My Lady at Last. A new Tale by the author of " The Last of th
Catholic O'Malleys." Crown 8vo., 5s.
" In the simple style in which it is narrated lies its charm."—*Athenæum.*

Out in the Cold World. By M. F. S., Author of "Fluffy,'
" Tom's Crucifix," " Catherine Hamilton." 3s. 6d.

The Rose of Venice. A tale of persecution by the Council of Te
in the old Venetian Republic. By S. Christopher. Crown 8vo., 5

Child's Picture Prayer Book. Sixteen tinted Illustration
cloth, 1s. and 1s. 6d. ; with coloured Illustrations, 1s. 6d., 2s.
2s. 6d., 3s., and 3s. 6d. French morocco, 3s. 6d. and 4s. Cal
5s. and 6s.

True Wayside Tales. By Lady Herbert. Foolscap 8vo., 3s.
or cheap edition, in 5 vols., in pretty binding, price 6d. each.
   1. **The Brigand Chief,** and other Tales.
   2. **Now is the Accepted Time,** and other Tales.
   3. **What a Child can do,** and other Tales.
   4. **Sowing Wild Oats,** and other Tales.
   5. **The Two Hosts,** and other Tales.

Chats about the Commandments. By Miss Plues, Author c
"Chats about the Rosary." 3s.

Little Books of St. Nicholas. By Rev. F. Drew. Fcap. 8vo., 1
   Ave Maria ; or Catesby's Story. [each.
   Credo ; or, Justin's Martyrdom.
   Veni Creator ; or, Ulrich's Money.
   Per Jesum Christum ; or, Two Good Fridays. .
   Pater Noster ; or, an Orphan Boy.
   Dominus Vobiscum ; or, The Sailor Boy.
   Oremus ; or, Little Mildred.

CATHOLIC PROGRESS. A Monthly Magazine. New an
enlarged series, 3d., post free, 4d. ; yearly subscription, 4s.

Indulgences, Sacramental Absolutions, and the Tax Tabl
of the Roman Chancery and Penitentiary considered. By the Re
T. L. Green, D.D. New Edition, with Index., 2s. 6d.

The Jesuits. By Paul Feval. English Translation. 12mo., 3s. 6

The Catholic Pilgrim's Progress—Sophia and Eulalie. Tran
lated from the French by George Ambrose Bradbury, O.C
Permissu Superiorum. 3s. 6d. ; cheaper edition, 1s. 6d.

Walter Ferrers' School Days ; or, Bellevue and its Owners. .
Tale for Boys. By C. Pilley. 2s. ; cheap edition, 1s.

OREMUS, A Liturgical Prayer Book : with the Imprimat
of the Cardinal Archbishop of Westminster. 32mo., 452 pag
paper cover, 2s. ; cloth, 2s. 6d. ; embossed, red edges, 3s. 6
French morocco, 4s. 6d. ; calf or morocco, 6s.; Russia, 8s. 6
Also in superior and more expensive bindings.

A Smaller Oremus ; an abridgment of the above. Cloth, 9d
with red edges, 1s. ; roan or French morocco, 2s. ; calf or m
rocco, 3s.; russia, 6s. Also in superior and more expensive binding
   ⁎ Specimen copy sent free on receipt of 1d. stamp.

The Child of Mary's Manual. Compiled from the Frenc
Second Edition, with Imprimatur. 1s.

R. Washbourne, 18 Paternoster Row, London.

Bluebeard ; or, the Key of the Cellar. A Drama in 3 Acts. 6d.
The Violet Sellers ; or, Kindness costs Little and is worth Much. Drama in 3 Acts for Children. 6d.
The Enchanted Violin. A Comedy in 2 Acts for Boys. 6d.
Nellie Gordon, the Factory Girl ; or, Lost and Saved. 6d.
Bertram Eldon, and how he found a Home. By the author of "Nellie Gordon." 1s.
Gathered Gems from Spanish Authors. By Mariana Monteiro, author of "The Monk of the Monastery of Yuste." 3s.

A DELSTAN'S (COUNTESS), Life and Letters. From the French of the Rev. Père Marquigny, S.J., 2s. 6d. ; cheap edition, 1s.
Adolphus ; or, the Good Son. 18mo., 6d.
Adventures of a Protestant in Search of a Religion By Iota. 12mo., 2s. and 3s. 6d.
Agnes Wilmott's History, and the Lessons it Taught. By M. A. Pennell, author of "Bertram Eldon," "Nellie Gordon," &c. 1s. 6d.
AGNEW (E.), Geraldine ; a Tale of Conscience. 3s. 6d.
Aikenhead (Mary), Life of. Giving a History of the Foundation of the Congregation of the Irish Sisters of Charity. 7s. 6d.
A'KEMPIS—Following of Christ. Dr. Challoner's Edition, 32mo., 1s.; embossed red edges, 1s. 6d. ; roan, 2s.; French morocco. 2s. 6d. ; calf or morocco, 4s. 6d. ; gilt, 5s. 6d. ; russia, 7s. 6d., 9s. and 12s. ; ivory, with rims and clasp, 15s., 16s., 18s.; mor. antique, with corners and clasps, 17s. 6d. ; russia, ditto, ditto, 16s. 20s.,
————— with Reflections. 32mo., 1s.; Persian, 3s. 6d. ; 12mo., 3s. 6d.; Persian, 7s. 6d.; mor., 9s.; mor. ant. 15s. ; Russia, 25s.
————— The Three Tabernacles. 16mo., 2s. 6d.
Albertus Magnus. By Rev. Fr. Dixon. 10s. 6d. ; cheap ed., 5s.
Allah Akbar—God is Great. An Arab Legend of the Siege and Conquest of Granada. From the Spanish. By Mariana Monteiro. 12mo., 3s. 6d.
ALLIES (T. W.), St. Peter; his Name and his Office. 5s.
Alphabet of Scripture Subjects. On a large sheet, 6d.; coloured, 1s., mounted to fold as a book, 2s. 6d.
ALZOG'S Church History. 8vo. 4 Vols. 7s. 6d. each.
AMHERST (Rt. Rev. Dr.), Lenten Thoughts. 1s. ; stronger bound, 2s., with red edges, 2s. 6d.
ANDERDON (Rev. W. H., S.J.), To Rome and Back. Fly-Leaves from a Flying Tour. 12mo., 2s.
ANDERSEN (Carl), Three Sketches of Life in Iceland. Translated by Myfanwy Fenton. 2s., cheap edition, 1s. 6d.
Angela Merici (S.) Her Life, her Virtues, and her Institute. From the French of the Abbé G. Beetemé. 12mo., 3s.
Angela's (S.) Manual : a Book of Devout Prayers and Exercises for Female Youth. Cloth, 2s.; Persian, 3s. 6d.; morocco, 4s.
Angels (The) and the Sacraments. Fcap 8vo., 1s. ; gilt, 1s. 6d.
————— Month of the Holy Angels. By Abbé Ricard. 1s.
Anglican Orders. By Canon Williams. 12mo., 3s. 6d.
Anglicanism, Harmony of. By T. M. W. Marshall. 2s. 6d.
Are You Safe in the Church of England? A Question for Anxious Ritualists. By Charles Walker, of Brighton. 8vo., 6d.

ARNOLD (Miss M. J.), Personal Recollections of Cardinal Wiseman, with other Memories. 12mo., 2s. 6d.

ARRAS (Madame d') The Two Friends; or Marie's Self-Denial. 12mo., 1s.; gilt edges, 1s. 6d.

Artist of Collingwood. 12mo., 1s.

Association of Prayers. By Rev. C. Tondini. 3d.

Aunt Margaret's Little Neighbours; or, Chats about the Rosary. By Miss Plues. 12mo., 3s.

Ave Maria; or Catesby's Story. By Rev. F. Drew. 1s.

BAGSHAWE(Rev. J. B.), The Credentials of the Catholic Church. 12mo., 4s.

———— **Threshold of the Catholic Church.** A Course of Plain Instructions for those entering her Communion. 12mo., 4s.

BAGSHAWE (Rt. Rev. Dr.), The Life of Our Lord, commemorated in the Mass. 18mo., 1s.

BAKER (Fr., O.S.B.), The Rule of S. Benedict. From the old English edition of 1638. 12mo., 4s. 6d.

Baker (Fr. Augustine, O.S.B.), Life and Spirit of. 2s. 6d.

Baker's Boy; or, Life of General Drouot. 18mo., 6d.

BALDESCHI. Ceremonial according to the Roman Rite. Translated by Rev. J. D. Hilarius Dale. 12mo., 6s. 6d.

BALMES (J.L.), Letters to a Sceptic. 12mo., 3s. 6d.

BAMPFIELD (Rev. G.), Sir Ælfric and other Tales. 18mo., 6d.; cloth, 1s.; gilt, 1s. 6d.

BARGE (Rev. T.), Occasional Prayers for Festivals. 32mo., 4d. and 6d.; gilt, 1s.

Battista Varani (B.), *see* Veronica (S.). 12mo., 5s.

Battle of Connemara. By Kathleen O'Meara. 12mo., 3s.

BAUGHAN (Rosa), Shakespeare's Tragedies and Comedies. Expurgated edition. 8vo., 6s. The Comedies only, 3s. 6d.

Before the Altar. 32mo., 6d.

Beleaguered Hearth (The). A Novel. 12mo., 2s. 6d.

BELL'S Modern Reader and Speaker. 12mo., 3s. 6d.

———— **Theory of Elocution.** 3s. 6d.

BELLECIUS (Fr.), Spiritual Exercises of S. Ignatius. 2s.

———— **Solid Virtue.** New edition. 12mo., 7s. 6d.

Bellevue and its Owners. A Tale for Boys. By C. Pilley. 2s. and 1s.

BELLINGHAM (Lady Constance) The Duties of Christian Parents. Conferences by Père Matignon. Translated with a Preface by the Rt. Rev. Mgr. Capel, D.D. 12mo., 5s.

Bells of the Sanctuary,—A Daughter of St. Dominick. By Grace Ramsay. 12mo., 1s. and 1s. 6d.; stronger bound, 2s.

BENEDICT (S.), The Rule of our most Holy Father S. Benedict, Patriarch of Monks. From the old English edition of 1638, Edited in Latin and English by one of the Benedictine Fathers of St. Michael's, near Hereford. 12mo., 4s. 6d.

Benedict's (S.) Manual. 18mo., 3s.

———— **Life and Miracles.** By S. Gregory the Great. From an old English version. By P. W. (Paris, 1608). Edited by Dom E. J. Luck, O.S.B. 4to. cloth, extra gilt, with 52 large Photographs, 31s. 6d.; or without the Photos., 10s. 6d. A small edition in fcap. 8vo. 2s.; or in stronger binding, 2s. 6d.

BENNI (Most Rev. C. B.), Tradition of the Syriac Church, concerning the Primacy and Prerogatives of S. Peter. 8vo., 7s. 6d.

Benvenuto Bambozzi (Fr., O.M.C.), of the Conventual Friars Minor, Life of, from the Italian (2nd edition) of Fr. Nicholas Treggiari, D.D. 12mo., 5s.

Berchmans (Bl. John), New Miracle at Rome, through the intercession of Bl. John Berchmans. 12mo., 2d.

Bernardine (St.) of Siena, Life of. With Portrait. 12mo., 5s.

Bertram Eldon, and how he found a Home. By M. A. Pennell, author of "Nellie Gordon" (6d), "Agnes Wilmott's History" (1s. 6d.). 12mo., 1s.

Bessy ; or, the Fatal Consequence of Telling Lies. By Miss K. M. Weld. 12mo., 1s.; stronger bound, 1s. 6d.; gilt, 2s.

BESTE (J. R. Digby), Catholic Hours. 2s. 6d. ; morocco, 6s.

———— **Holy Readings.** 2s. and 2s. 6d. ; roan, 3s. ; mor., 6s.

BESTE (Rev. Fr.), Victories of Rome. 8vo., 1s.

BETHELL (Rev. A.), Our Lady's Month ; or, Short Lessons for the Month of May, and the Feasts of Our Lady. 18mo., 1s., stronger bound, 1s. 6d.

Bible. Douay Version. 12mo., 3s. ; Persian, 8s. ; morocco, 10s. 6d. 18mo., 2s. 6d. ; Persian, 5s.; calf or morocco, 7s. ; gilt, 8s. 6d. Large 18mo., cloth, 6s ; Persian, 8s. and 9s.; morocco, 11s. 6d. With borders round pages, 8vo., cloth, 8s. ; Persian calf, 21s. ; morocco, 25s. 4to., cloth, 21s.; leather extra, 31s. 6d. Illustrated, morocco, £5 5s.; superior, £6 6s.

Bible History for the use of Schools. By Abp. Gilmour. 2s.

Bible History, Catholic Child's. 9d. O. T., 3d.; N. T., 3d.

Blessed Lord. *See* Ribadeneira, 1s. ; Rutter (Rev. H.)., 5s.

Blessed Virgin, Devotions to. From Ancient Sources. *See* Regina Sæculorum. 12mo., 3s. ; cheap edition, 1s.

———— **History of.** By Orsini. Translated by Provost Husenbeth. Illustrated, 12mo., 3s. 6d.

———— **Life of.** In verse. By C. E. Tame, Esq. 16mo., 2s.

———— **Life of.** Proposed as a model to Christian women. 12mo., 1s.

———— **in North America, Devotion to.** By Fr. Macleod. 5s.

———— **Veneration of.** By Mrs. Stuart Laidlaw. 16mo., 4d.

———— *See* Our Lady, p. 22 ; Leaflets, p. 16 ; May, p. 19.

Blindness, Cure of, through the Intercession of Our Lady and S. Ignatius. 12mo., 2d.

BLOSIUS, Spiritual Works of :—The Rule of the Spiritual Life ; The Spiritual Mirror ; String of Spiritual Jewels. Edited by Rev. Fr. John Bowden. 12mo., 3s. 6d.; red edges, 4s.

Blue Scapular, Origin of. 18mo., 1d.

Bluebeard ; or, the Key of the Cellar. A Drama in 3 Acts. 6d.

BLYTH (Rev. Fr.), Devout Paraphrase on the Seven Penitential Psalms. To which is added "Necessity of Purifying the Soul," by S. Francis de Sales. 18mo., 1s. stronger bound, 1s. 6d.; red edges, 2s.

Bobbie and Birdie ; or, Our Lady's Picture. A Story for the very little ones. By Frances J. M. Kershaw. 2s. 6d.

BONA (Cardinal), Easy Way to God. Translated by Father Collins. 12mo., 3s.

BONAVENTURE (S.), Life of St. Francis of Assisi. Translated from the Italian by the author of "The Life of St. Teresa" (Miss Lockhart). 3s. 6d.

Boniface (S.), Life of. By Mrs. Hope. 12mo., 6s.

BOUDON (Mgr.), Book of Perpetual Adoration. Translated by Rev. Dr. Redman. 12mo., 3s.; red edges, 3s. 6d.

BOUDREAUX (Rev. J., S.J.), God our Father. 12mo., 4s.

BOWDEN (Rev. Fr. John), Spiritual Works of Louis of Blois. 12mo., 3s. 6d.

———Oratorian Lives of the Saints. (Page 22).

BOWDEN (Mrs.), Lives of the First Religious of the Visitation of Holy Mary. 2 vols., 12mo., 10s.

BOWLES (Emily), Eagle and Dove. Translated from the French of Mdlle. Zénaïde Fleuriot. 12mo., 2s. 6d. and 5s.

BRADBURY (Rev. Fr.), Sophia and Eulalie. (The Catholic Pilgrim's Progress). 12mo., 1s. 6d.; better bound, 3s. 6d.

BRICKLEY'S Standard Table Book. 32mo., ½d.

BRIDGES (Miss), Sir Thomas Maxwell and his Ward. 1s.

Bridget (S.), Life of, and other Saints of Ireland. 12mo., 1s.

Brigit (S.) Life of, &c. By M. F. Cusack. 8vo., 6s.

Broken Chain. A Tale. 18mo., 6d.

BROWNE (E. G. K., Esq.), Monastic Legends. 8vo., 6d.

BROWNLOW (Rev. W. R. B.), Church of England and its Defenders. 8vo., 1st letter, 6d.; 2nd letter, 1s.

——— ——— "Vitis Mystica"; or, the True Vine: a Treatise on the Passion of our Lord. 18mo., 4s.; red edges, 4s. 6d.

BUCKLEY (Rev. M.), Sermons, Lectures, &c. 12mo., 6s.

BULENS (F. Alexis, of the Monastery, West Gorton), Treatise on the Way of Sorrows, followed by a Practical Method of Blessing, Erecting, and Solemnly Performing the Stations of the Way of the Cross. 1s. 6d.; red edges, &c., 2s.

BURDER (Abbot), Confidence in the Mercy of God. By Mgr. Languet. 12mo., 3s.

——— The Consoler; or, Pious Readings addressed to the Sick and all who are afflicted. By Père Lambilotte. 4s. 6d.; red edges, 5s.

——— Souls in Purgatory. 32mo., 3d.

Burial of the Dead. For Children and Adults. (Latin and English.) Clear type edition, 32mo., 6d.; roan, 1s. 6d.

BURKE (Rev. T. N.), Lectures and Sermons. 3 vols., 36s.

BURKE (James), Travels of an Irish Gentleman in search of a Religion. 12mo., 3s. 6d.

BUTLER (Alban), Lives of the Saints. 2 vols., 8vo., 28s.; gilt, 34s.; 4 vols., 8vo., 32s.; gilt, 50s.; leather, 64s.

——— One Hundred Pious Reflections. 18mo., 1s. and 2s.

BUTLER (Dr.), Catechisms. 1st, ½d.; 2nd, 1d.; 3rd, 1½d.

CALIXTE—Life of the Ven. Anna Maria Taigi. Translated by A. V. Smith Sligo. 8vo., 2s. 6d. and 5s.

Callista. Dramatised by Dr. Husenbeth. 12mo., 2s.

CAMERON (Marie), The Golden Thought, and other Stories. 12mo. 1s. 6d.; gilt, 2s.; or cheap edition, separately, 6d. each.
  1. The Golden Thought, and The Brother's Grave.
  2. The Rod that bore Blossoms, and Patience and Impatience.

CARAHER (Hugh), A Month at Lourdes and its Neighbourhood. Two Illustrations. 12mo., 2s.

Catechisms—The Catechism of Christian Doctrine. *New edition*, No. 1, ½d., or 3s. a 100 ; No. 2, 1d. or 6s. a 100.
————— *The Old edition of No. 2, is offered at Half Price.*
————— made Easy. By Rev. H. Gibson. Vol. III., 4s.
————— By Fr. Power. 3 vols., 10s. 6d. ; 2 vols., 7s. 6d.
————— By Dr. Butler. 32mo., 1st, ½d.; 18mo., 2nd, 1d.; 3rd, 1½d.
————— By Dr. Doyle. 18mo., 1½d.
————— By Bishop Challoner. Grounds of Catholic Doctrine. 4d.
————— Fleury's Historical. Complete Edition. 18mo., 1½d.
————— Frassinetti's Dogmatic. 12mo., 3s.
————— Keenan's Controversial. 2s.
————— Lessons on Christian Doctrine. 18mo., 1½d.
————— for First Confession. By Rev. R. G. Davis, 1d.
————— of Confirmation. A very complete book. 18mo., 3d.
————— of Perseverance. By Gaume. Vols. I. to III., 7s. 6d. each.
————— of the Council. 12mo., 3d.
————— of the History of England. By a Lady. 18mo., 1s.
————————— for the Use of Pupil Teachers. 6d.

Catherine Hamilton. By M. F. S. 12mo., 2s. 6d.; gilt, 3s.
Catherine Grown Older. By M. F. S. 12mo., 2s. 6d.; gilt, 3s.
Catholic Calendar for England. 6d. ; Almanack, 1d.
Catholic Directory for Scotland. 1s.
Catholic Hours. By J. R. Digby Beste. 2s. 6d.
Catholic Piety. *See* Prayer Books, page 31.
Catholic Pilgrim's Progress—The Journey of Sophia and Eulalie to the Palace of True Happiness. 2s. 6d. Cheap edition, 1s. 6d.
Catholic Progress. A Monthly Magazine. Price 3d.
Catholic Sick and Benefit Club. By Rev. R. Richardson. 4d.
Ceremonies of Low Mass. 2s. 6d.
CHALLONER (Dr.), Grounds of Catholic Doctrine. 4d.
————— Think Well on't. 18mo., 2d.; cloth, 6d.
Chats about the Rosary. By Miss Plues. 3s.
Chats about the Commandments. By the same. 3s.
CHAUGY (Mother Frances Magdalen de), Lives of the First Religious of the Visitation. 2 vols., 12mo., 10s.
Child's Book of the Passion of Our Lord. 32mo., 6d.
Child (The) of Mary's Manual. Second edition, 32mo. 1s.
Child's Picture Prayer Book. With 16 Illustrations. Cloth, tinted, 1s. and 1s. 6d. ; coloured, 1s. 6d., 2s., 2s. 6d., 3s., 3s. 6d. French morocco, 3s. 6d. and 4s. Calf, 5s. and 6s.
Children of Mary Card of Enrolment. Folio, 9d., post free on a roller, 1s.
Children of Mary in the World, Rules of. 32mo., 1d.
Christ bearing His Cross. A Steel Engraving from the Picture miraculously given to Blessed Colomba, with a short account of her Life. 8vo., 6d.; proofs, 1s.
Christian Doctrine, Lessons on. 18mo., 1½d.
Christian, Duties of a. By Ven. de la Salle. 12mo., 2s.
Christian Politeness. By the same Author. 18mo., 1s.
Christmas (The First) for our dear Little Ones. 4to., 6s.
CHRISTOPHER (S.) The Rose of Venice. A Tale. 5s.
Chronological Sketches. By H. Murray Lane. 2s. 6d.

Church Defence. By T. W. M. Marshall. 2s. 6d.

Church of England and its Defenders. 1s.

Cistercian Legends of the XIII. Century. 3s.

Cistercian Order : its Mission and Spirit. 3s. 6d.

Clare (Sister Mary Cherubini) of S. Francis, Life of. Preface by Lady Herbert. With Portrait. 12mo., 3s. 6d.

Clare's Sacrifice. By C. M. O'Hara. A Tale for First Communicants. 6d.

Cloister Legends ; or, Convents and Monasteries in the Olden Time. 12mo., 4s.

COBBETT'S History of the Protestant Reformation. 4s. 6d.

COLLINS (Rev. Fr.), Legends of the XIII. Century. 12mo., 3s., or in 3 vols., 1s. 6d. each.

———— **Cistercian Order : its Mission and Spirit.** 3s. 6d.

———— **Easy Way to God.** Translated from the Latin of Cardinal Bona. 12mo., 3s.

———— **Spiritual Conferences on the Mysteries of Faith and the Interior Life.** 12mo., 5s.

COLOMBIERE (Father Claude de la), The Sufferings of Our Lord. Sermons preached in the Chapel Royal, St. James's, in the year 1677. Preface by Fr. Doyotte, S.J. 18mo., 1s. ; stronger bound, 1s. 6d. ; red edges, 2s.

Colombini (B. Giovanni), Life of. By Belcari. Translated from the editions of 1541 and 1832. With Portrait. 12mo., 3s. 6d.

Comedy of Convocation in the English Church. Edited by Archdeacon Chasuble. 8vo., 2s. 6d. *See* page 18.

COMERFORD (Rev. P.). Month of May for all the Faithful ; or, a Practical Life of the Blessed Virgin. 32mo., 1s.

———— **Pleadings of the Sacred Heart.** 18mo., 1s.; gilt, 2s.; with the Handbook of the Confraternity, 1s. 6d. Hand-book, 3d.

Communion, Manual for. Meditations and Prayers. 2s. 6d.

Communion, Prayers for, for Children. Preparation, Mass before Communion, Thanksgiving. 32mo. 1d.

Compendious Statement of the Scripture Doctrine regarding the Nature and chief Attributes of the Kingdom of Christ. By C. F. A. 8vo., 1s.

COMPTON (Herbert), Semi-Tropical Trifles. 12mo., boards, 1s.; extra cloth, 2s. 6d.

Conferences. *See* Collins, Lacordaire, Mermillod, Matignon, Ravignan.

Confession and Holy Communion : Young Catholic's Guide. By Dr. Kenny. 32mo., 4d.; cloth, 6d.; red edges, 9d., French morocco, 1s. 6d.; calf or morocco, 2s. 6d.

Confidence in the Mercy of God. By Mgr. Languet. Translated by Abbot Burder. 12mo., 3s.

Confirmation, Instructions for the Sacrament of. A very complete book. 3d.

———— **Order of Administering.** 3d.

Consoler (The). By Abbot Burder. 12mo., 4s. 6d. and 5s.

Contemplations on the Most Holy Sacrament of the Altar ; or Devout Meditations to serve as Preparations for, and Thanksgiving after, Communion. 1s. and 2s. ; red edges, 2s. 6d.

Conversion of the Teutonic Race. By Mrs. Hope. 2 vols. 10s.

Convert Martyr; or, "Callista." By the Rev. Dr. Newman, Dramatised by the Rev. Dr. Husenbeth. 12mo., 2s.
Convocation, Comedy of. By A. J. P. Marshall. 8vo. 2s. 6d.
CORTES (John Donoso), Essays on Catholicism, Liberalism, and Socialism. 12mo., 5s.
Credentials of the Catholic Church. By Rev. J. B. Bagshawe, author of " The Threshold of the Catholic Church." 12mo., 4s.
Crucifixion, The. A large Picture for School walls, 1s.
CULPEPPER. Family Herbal, 3s. 6d. ; coloured plates, 5s. 6d.
CUSACK (M. F.):—Sister Mary Francis Clare.
  Book of the Blessed Ones. 12mo., 4s. 6d.
  Case of Ireland Stated. 7s. 6d.
  Devotions for Public and Private Use at the Way of the Cross. Illustrated. 32mo., 1s.; red edges, 1s. 6d.
  Father Mathew, Life of. 12mo., 2s. 6d.
  Good Reading for Sundays and Festivals. 2s 6d.
  Handmaid of the Holy Ghost. 6d.
  History of the Irish Nation. Morocco gilt, 45s.
  Ireland, History of. 18mo., 2s.
  Jesus and Jerusalem. 4s. 6d.
  Jubilee of 1881. 3d.
  Knock ; Apparitions, &c. 1s.
  Knock : Three Visits to. 2s.
  Life of the Blessed Virgin, 12s.
  Life and Times of the Liberator. 2 vols., 16s.
  Life of Most Rev. Dr. Dixon. 7s. 6d.
  Life of Mary O'Hagan. 6s.
  Lives of St. Columba and St. Brigit. 8vo., 6s.
  Meditations for Advent, 3s. 6d.
  Ned Rusheen ; or, Who fired the first Shot. 5s.
  Nun's Advice to her Girls. 12mo., 2s. 6d.
  Patrick (S.), Life of. 8vo., 6s., gilt, 10s. ; 32mo. 1s.
  Patrick's (S.) Manual. 18mo., 3s. 6d.
  Pilgrim's Way to Heaven. 12mo., 4s. 6d.
  Retreat for the Three Last Days of the Year. 1s.
  The Spouse of Christ. 12mo., vol. 2, 7s. 6d.
  Tim O'Halloran's Choice. 12mo., 3s. 6d.
  Tronson's Conferences. 12mo., 4s. 6d.
  Woman's Work in Modern Society. 4s. 6d.
DALE (Rev. J. D. H.), Sacristan's Manual. 12mo., 2s. 6d.
Dark Shadow (The). A Tale. 12mo., 3s.
Daughter (A) of S. Dominick : (Bells of the Sanctuary). By Grace Ramsay. 12mo., 1s. and 1s. 6d. ; better bound, 2s.
·DAVIS (Rev. R. G.) Garden of the Soul. *See* pages 30 and 32.
——— **Catechism for First Confession.** 1d
DECHAMPS (Mgr.), The Life of Pleasure. 12mo., 1s. 6d.
DEHAM (Rev. F.) Sacred Heart of Jesus, offered to the Piety of the Young engaged in Study. 32mo., 9d.
Diary of a Confessor of the Faith. 12mo., 1s.
Directorium Asceticum. By Scaramelli. 4 vols., 12mo., 24s.
DIXON (Fr., O.P.) Albertus Magnus: his Life and Scholastic Labours. From original documents. By Dr. Sighart. With Photographic Portrait. 8vo. 10s. 6d. Cheap edition, 5s.

DIXON (Fr., O.P.) **Life of St. Vincent Ferrer.** From the French of Rev. Fr. Pradel. With a Photograph. 12mo., 5s.

Dominican Saints, Sketches of the Lives of. By M. K. 3s. 6d.

Dominus Vobiscum ; or, the Sailor Boy. By Rev. F. Drew. 1s.

DOWNING (Sister M. A.), Voices from the Heart. 2s. 6d.

DOYLE (Canon, O.S.B.), Life of Gregory Lopez, the Hermit. With a Photographic Portrait. 12mo., 3s. 6d.

———— **Lectures for Boys.** 2 Vols., 12mo., 10s. 6d. ; or separately :—Vol. I., Containing—The Sundays of the Year, and Our Lady's Festivals, etc. 6s.—Vol. II., Containing—The Passion of Our Lord, and The Sacred Heart. 6s. ; or may be had separately : The Sundays of the Year, 3s. 6d. ; Our Lady's Festivals, etc., 2s. 6d. ; The Passion of Our Lord, 3s. ; The Sacred Heart, 3s.

———— **Rule of our holy Father St. Benedict.** Edited in Latin and English. 12mo., 4s. 6d.

DOYLE (Dr.), Catechism. 18mo., 1½d.

DOYOTTE (Fr., S.J.), Elevations to the Heart of Jesus. 3s.

———— **Sufferings of Our Lord.** By Fr. Columbiere. 1s.

DRAMAS. Bluebeard ; or, the Key of the Cellar. A Drama in 3 Acts. 6d.

———— **Convert Martyr ;** or, "Callista" dramatised. 2s.

———— **The Duchess Transformed** (Girls, 1 Act). Comedy. 6d.

———— **The Enchanted Violin** (Boys, 2 Acts). Comedy. 6d.

———— **Ernscliff Hall** (Girls, 3 Acts). Drama. 12mo., 6d.

———— **Filiola** (Girls, 4 Acts). Drama. 12mo., 6d.

———— **Finola** (Moore Melodies, 4 Acts). An Opera. 1s.

———— **He would be a Lord** (Boys, 3 Acts), a Comedy. 2s.

———— **He would be a Soldier** (Boys, 2 Acts) Comedy, 6d.

———— **Reverse of the Medal** (Girls, 4 Acts). Drama. 6d.

———— **Shakespeare.** Expurgated Edition. 8vo., 6s.

———— **Shandy Maguire** (Boys, 2 Acts), a Farce. 12mo., 2s.

———— **St. Eustace** (Boys, 5 Acts). Drama. 12mo., 1s.

———— **St. William of York** (Boys, 2 Acts). Drama. 12mo., 6d.

———— **The Violet Sellers** (3 Acts). Drama for Children. 6d.

———— **Whittington and his Cat.** Drama for Children. 9 Scenes. By Henrietta Fairfield. 6d.

———— *See* R. Washbourne's **American List.**

DRANE (Augusta Theodosia), Inner Life of Pere Lacordaire. Translated from the French of Père Chocarne. 6s. 6d.

DREW (Rev. F.), Little Books of St. Nicholas. Tales for Children, 1s. each. 1. Oremus ; 2. Dominus Vobiscum ; 3. Pater Noster. 4. Per Jesum Christi ; 5. Veni Creator ; 6. Credo ; 7. Ave Maria ; 8. Ora pro nobis : 9. Corpus Christi ; 10. Dei Genitrix ; 11. Miserere ; 12. Deo Gratias ; 13. Angelus Domini.

Duchess (The), Transformed. By W. H. A. 12mo., 6d.

DUMESNIL (Abbe), The Reign of Terror. 12mo., 2s. 6d.

DUPANLOUP (Mgr.), Contemporary Prophecies. 8vo., 1s.

———— **The Child.** Translated by Kate Anderson. 12mo., 3s. 6d.

Dusseldorf Gallery. 357 Engravings. Large 4to. Half-morocco gilt, £5 5s. nett.

———— 134 Engravings. Large 8vo. Half-morocco, gilt, 42s.

Dusseldorf Society for the Distribution of Good Religious Pictures. Subscription, 8s. 6d. a year.

Duties of Christian Parents. Conferences by R. Père Matignon Translated from the French by Lady Constance Bellingham. 5s.

Eagle and Dove. Translated by Emily Bowles. 5s. and 2s. 6d.

Easy Way to God. By Cardinal Bona. 12mo., 3s.

Electricity and Magnetism; an Enquiry into the Nature and Results of. By Amyclanus. Illustrated. 12mo., 6s. 6d.

Enchanted Violin, The. A Comedy in 2 Acts (Boys), 6d.

England, History of. By L. Evans. St. 3, 2d. ; 4, 2d. ; 5, 3d.

———— A Catechism. For the use of Pupil Teachers, 6d. By a Teacher, 1s. By a Lady, 6d.

———— By W. F. Mylius. 12mo., 3s. 6d.

Epistles and Gospels. Good clear type edition, 32mo., 6d.; roan, 1s. 6d.; larger edition, 18mo., French morocco, 2s.

————, **Explanation of.** By Rev. F. Goffine. Illustrated, 8vo., 9s.

Ernscliff Hall. A Drama in Three Acts, for Girls. 12mo., 6d.

Eucharistic Year. 18mo., 4s.

Eucharist (The) and the Christian Life. 3s. 6d.

Eustace (St.). A Drama in 5 Acts for Boys. 12mo., 1s.

EVANS (L.), History of England, adapted for Junior Classes in Schools. Part 1 (Standard 3) 2d. Part 2 (Standard 4) 2d. Part 3 (Standard 5) 3d.

———— Chronological Outline of English History. 1½d.

———— Milton's l'Allegro (Oxford Local Exam.). 2d.

———— Parsing and Analysis Table. 1d.

FAIRFIELD (Henrietta), Whittington and his Cat. A Drama, in 9 Scenes, for Children. 12mo., 6d.

Fairy Ching (The); or, the Chinese Fairies' Visit to England. By Henrica Frederic. 12mo., 1s. ; gilt edges, 1s. 6d.

Fairy Tales for Little Children. By Madeleine Howley Meehan, 12mo., 6d.; stronger bound, 1s. and 1s. 6d.; gilt, 2s.

Faith, Hope, and Charity; a Tale of the Reign of Terror. 2s. 6d.

Faith of our Fathers. By Most Rev. Archbishop Gibbons. 4s.

Fall, Redemption, and Exaltation of Man. 12mo., 1s.

Familiar Instructions on Christian Truths. By a Priest. 10d.

Fardel (Sister Claude Simplicienne), Life of. With the Lives of others of the First Religious of the Visitation of Holy Mary. 12mo., 6s.

FARRELL (Rev. J.), Lectures of a certain Professor. 7s. 6d

FAVRE (Abbe), Heaven Opened by the Practice of Frequent Confession and Communion. 12mo., 2s. ; stronger bound, 3s. 6d.

Favre (Mother Marie Jacqueline), Life of. With the Lives of others of the First Religious of the Visitation of Holy Mary. 12mo., 6s.

Feasts (The) of Camelot, with the Tales that were told there. By Mrs. E. L. Hervey. 3s. 6d., or in 2 vols. 1s. 6d. each.

FERRIS (Rev. D.), Life of Sister Mary Frances of the Five Wounds. From the Italian. 12mo., 2s. 6d.

———— Manual of Christian Doctrine ; or Catholic Belief and Practice familiary explained by Question and Answer. 6d.

FEVAL (Paul), The Jesuits. Translated from the French. 3s. 6d.

Filiola. A Drama in Four Acts, for Girls. 12mo., 6d.

First Apostles of Europe. By Mrs. Hope. 2 vols. 10s.

First Communion and Confirmation Memorial. Beautifully printed in gold and colours, folio, 1s. each, or 9s. a dozen, nett.

First Communion ; or, Clare's Sacrifice. By O'Hara. 6d.

First Religious of the Visitation of Holy Mary, Lives of. Translated, with a Preface, by Mrs. Bowden. 2 vols., 10s.

FLANAGAN (Rev. T.), History of the Catholic Church in England. 2 vols., 8vo., 18s.

FLEET (Charles), Tales and Sketches. 8vo., 3s. 6d.

FLEURIOT (Mlle. Zenaïde), Eagle and Dove. Translated by Emily Bowles. 12mo., 2s. 6d. and 5s.

FLEURY'S Historical Catechism. Large edition, 12mo., 1½d.

Flowers of Christian Wisdom. By Henry Lucien. 2s.

Fluffy. A Tale for Boys. By M. F. S. 12mo., 3s. 6d.

Following of Christ. *See* A'Kempis.

For Better, not for Worse. By Rev. Langton George Vere.

Foreign Books. *See* R. W.'s Catalogue of Foreign Books.

FORMBY (Rev. H.), Little Book of the Martyrs. 1s. 6d.

Francis of Assisi (S.) Life of. By S. Bonaventure. Translated by Miss Lockhart. 12mo., 3s. 6d.

———— Woks of. Translated by a Religious of the Order. 4s.

FRANCIS OF SALES (S.), Consoling Thoughts. 18mo., 2s.

———— The Mystical Flora. 4to., 6s.

———— Necessity of Purifying the Soul. By Fr. Blyth. 1s.

———— Sweetness of Holy Living. 1s.

Franciscan Annals and Monthly Bulletin of the Third Order of St. Francis 5s. year, post free.

FRANCO (Rev. S.) Devotions to the Sacred Heart. 4s.

FRASSINETTI—Dogmatic Catechism. 12mo., 3s.

FREDERIC (Henrica), The Fairy Ching ; or, the Chinese Fairies' Visit to England. 12mo., 1s.; gilt edges, 1s. 6d.

———— Story of a Paper Knife. 12mo., 1s.; gilt edges, 1s. 6d.

From Sunrise to Sunset. By L. B. 12mo., 3s. 6d.

GALLERY (Rev. D.), Handbook of Essentials in History and Literature, Ancient and Modern. 18mo., 1s. 6d.

Garden of the Soul. *See* page 32.

Garden (Little) of the Soul. *See* page 30.

Gathered Gems from Spanish Authors. By M. Monteiro. 3s.

GAUME (Abbe), Catechism of Perseverance. 4 vols., 12mo. Vols. 1, 2 and 3, each 7s. 6d.

GAYRARD (Mme. Paul) Harmony of the Passion. Compiled from the four Gospels, in Latin and French. 18mo., 1s. 6d.

German (S.), Life of. 12mo., 3s. 6d.

GIBBONS (Most Rev. Archbishop), The Faith of our Fathers; Being a Plain Exposition and Vindication of the Church Founded by our Lord Jesus Christ. 12mo., 4s. Paper covers, 2s.

GIBSON (Rev. H.), Catechism made Easy. Vol. III., 4s.

GILMOUR (Rev. R.), Bible History for the Use of Schools. Illustrated. 12mo., 2s.

God our Father. By a Father of the Society of Jesus. 12mo., 4s.

GOFFINE (Rev. F.), Explanation of the Epistles and Gospels. Illustrated. 8vo., 9s.

Golden Thought of Queen Beryl, and other Stories. By Marie Cameron. 1s. 6d. ; or cheap edition, in 2 vols. 6d. each.

Grace before and after Meals. 32mo., 1d. ; cloth, 2d.

GRACE RAMSAY. *See* O'Meara (Kathleen).

GRACIAN (Fr. Baltasar), Sanctuary Meditations for Priests and Frequent Communicants. Translated from the Spanish by Mariana Monteiro. 12mo., 4s.

Grains of Gold. Series 1 and 2, cloth, 2s. 6d., separately, 1s. each.

GRANT (Bishop), Pastoral on St. Joseph. 32mo., 4d. & 6d.

GRAY (Mrs. C. D.), Simple Bible Stories. 1s. and 2s. 6d.

GREEN (Rev. Dr.), Indulgences, Sacramental Absolutions, and the Tax Tables with New Preface and Index. 2s. 6d.

Gregory Lopez, the Hermit, Life of. By Canon Doyle, O.S.B. With a Photographic Portrait. 12mo., 3s. 6d.

Grounds of the Catholic Doctrine. By Bishop Challoner. Large type edition, 18mo., 4d.

GUERANGER (Dom), Defence of the Roman Church against F. Gratry. Translated by Canon Woods. 8vo., 1s.

Harmony of Anglicanism. By T. W. Marshall.. 8vo., 2s. 6d.

HAY (Bishop), Sincere Christian. 18mo., 2s. 6d.
———— Devout Christian. 18mo., 2s. 6d.

He would be a Lord. A Comedy in 3 Acts. (Boys.) 12mo., 2s.

Heart of Jesus at Nazareth. Meditations. 3s. 6d.

Heaven Opened by the Practice of frequent Confession and Holy Communion. By the Abbé Favre. 12mo., 2s. ; stronger bound, 3s. 6d.

HEDLEY (Bishop), Five Sermons—Light of the Holy Spirit in the World. 12mo., 1s.; cloth, 1s. 6d. Revelation, Mystery, Dogma and Creeds, Infallibility : separately, 3d. each.

HEFELE (Rev. Dr. Von), Cardinal Ximenes. 10s. 6d.

HEIGHAM (John), A Devout Exposition of the Holy Mass. Edited by Austin John Rowley, Priest. 12mo., 4s.

HENRY (Lucien), Flowers of Christian Wisdom. 18mo., 1s. and 2s.; red edges, 2s. 6d.

Herbal, Brook's Family. 12mo., 3s. 6d.; coloured, 5s. 6d.

HERBERT (Lady), True Wayside Tales. 12mo., 3s. ; or in 5 vols., cheap edition, 6d. each.

    1. The Brigand Chief, and other Tales. 2. Now is the Accepted Time, and other Tales. 3. What a Child can do, and other Tales. 4. Sowing Wild Oats, and other Tales. 5. The Two Hosts, and other Tales.
———— Second Series of True Wayside Tales. [*In the press.*]

HERBERT (Wallace), My Dream and other Verses. 5s.
———— The Angels and the Sacraments. 1s. ; gilt, 1s. 6d.

Hermann, Fr. (Carmelite), Life of. 8vo., 5s. 6d. ; better bound, 6s. 6d.

HERVEY (E. L.), Stories from many Lands. 12mo., 3s. 6d.
———— Our Legends and Lives. 12mo., 6s.
———— Rest, on the Cross. 12mo., 3s. 6d.
———— The Feasts of Camelot, with the Tales that were told there. 12mo., 3s. 6d. ; or, separately : Christmas, 1s. 6d. ; Whitsuntide, 1s. 6d.

HILL (Rev. Fr.), Elements of Philosophy, comprising Logic and General Principles of Metaphysics. 8vo., 6s.

—————— **Ethics, or Moral Philosophy.** 12mo., 6s.

HOFFMAN (Franz), Industry and Laziness. 12mo., 3s.

Holy Church the Centre of Unity. By T. H. Shaw. 1s.

Holy Communion. By Hubert Lebon. 12mo., 4s.

Holy Family Card of Membership. A beautiful design. Folio. Price 6d., or 8d., on a roller, post free ; 4s. 6d. a dozen, or post free 5s.

Holy Family, Confraternity of. By Card. Manning. 3d.

Holy Places : their Sanctity and Authenticity. 2s. 6d.

Holy Readings. By J. R. Digby Beste, Esq. 3s.

Holy Week Book. New edition, with Ordinary of the Mass, Vespers and Complin, Blessing of the Holy Oils, &c. 1s.

HOPE (Mrs.), The First Apostles of Europe ; or, "The Conversion of the Teutonic Race." 2 vols., 12mo., 10s.

Horace. Literally translated by Smart, 2s. Latin and English, 3s. 6d.

HUGUET (Pere), The Power of S. Joseph. 1s. 6d.

—————— **On Charity in Conversation.** 12mo., 2s. 6d.

HUMPHREY (Rev. W., S.J.), The Panegyrics of Fr. Segneri, S.J. Translated from the orignal Italian. With a Preface by the Rev. W. Humphrey, S.J. 12mo., 6s.

HUSENBETH (Rev. Dr.), Convert Martyr. 12mo., 2s.

—————— **History of the Blessed Virgin.** Translated from Orsini. Illustrated. 12mo., 3s. 6d.

—————— **Life and Sufferings of Our Lord.** By Rev. H. Rutter. Illustrated. 12mo., 5s.

—————— **Life of Mgr. Weedall.** 8vo., 5s.

—————— **Little Office of the Immaculate Conception.** In Latin and English. 32mo., 4d. ; cloth, 6d.; roan, 1s. ; calf or morocco, 2s. 6d.

—————— **Our Blessed Lady of Lourdes.** 18mo., 6d.; with the Novena, 1s.; cloth, 1s. 6d. Novena, separately, 4d.; Litany, 1d.

—————— **Roman Question.** 8vo., 6d.

HUTTON (Arthur W.), Vesper Psalms and Magnificat for all Sundays and Feast days throughout the year, set to harmonised Chants for alternate singing, with the Gregorian Tones. 3s. Nett, 10 copies for 25s.

Hymn Book (The Catholic). Edited by Rev. G. Langton Vere. 32mo., 1d. ; larger edition, 204 pages, 2d.; cloth, 4d.

Iceland (Three Sketches of Life in). By Carl Andersen. 12mo., 2s., cheap edition, 1s. 6d.

IGNATIUS (S.), Spiritual Exercises. By Fr. Bellecio, S.J. Translated by Dr. Hutch. 18mo., 2s.

Ignatius (S.), Cure of Blindness through the Intercession of Our Lady and S. Ignatius. 12mo., 2d.

Imitation of Christ. *See* A'Kempis.

Immaculate Conception, Definition of. 12mo., 6d.

—————— **Little Office of, Latin and English.** 32mo., 2d.

—————— **Little Office of.** By Rev. Dr. Husenbeth. 4d. ; cloth, 6d. ; roan, 1s.; calf or morocco, 2s. 6d.

Industry and Laziness. By Franz Hoffman. From the German, by James King. 12mo., 3s.

Indulgences. *See* Green, 2s. 6d.; Matthews, 1d.; Maurel, 2s.

Infallibility of the Pope. By the Author of "The Oxford Undergraduate of Twenty Years Ago." 8vo., 1s.

In Suffragiis Sanctorum. Commem. S. Joseph ; Commem. S. Georgii. Set of 5 for 4d.

IOTA. The Adventures of a Protestant in Search of a Religion : being the Story of a late Student of Divinity at Bunyan Baptist College ; a Nonconformist Minister, who seceded to the Catholic Church. 12mo., 3s. 6d. ; cheap edition, 2s.

Ireland (History of). By Miss Cusack. 2s. By T. Young. 2s. 6d.

Irish Board Reading Books.

Irish First Book. 18mo., 2d. **2nd Book,** 4d. **3rd Book,** 6d.

Irish Monthly. 8vo. Vol. 1882, cloth, 7s. 6d.

Irish Saints in Great Britain. By Bishop Moran. 5s.

Italian Revolution (The History of). The History of the Barricades. By Keyes O'Clery, M.P. 8vo., 7s. 6d. and 3s. 6d.

Jack's Boy. By M. F. S., author of "Fluffy." 12mo, 3s. 6d.

JACOB (W. J.), Personal Recollections of Rome. 6d.

Jesuits (The). By Paul Feval. Translated from the French, 3s. 6d.

Jesuits (The), and other Essays. By Willis Nevin. 2s. 6d.

Jesus and Jerusalem ; or, the Way Home. 4s. 6d.

Jew of Verona. 12mo., 4s. 6d.

John of God (S.), Life of. With Photographic Portrait. 12mo., 5s.

Joseph (S.), Life of. By Miss Cusack. 32mo., 6d.; cloth, 1s.

—————— **Manual of a Happy Eternity.** 18mo., 2s. 6d.

—————— **Novena of Meditations.** 18mo., 1s.

—————— **Novena to,** with a Pastoral by the late Bishop Grant. 32mo., 4d.; cloth, 6d.

—————— **Power of.** By Fr. Huguet. 1s. 6d.

—————— **A Word to,** for every day in March. 4d., cloth, 1s.

—————— *See* Leaflets.

Journey of Sophia and Eulalie to the Palace of True Happiness. (The Catholic Pilgrim's Progress.) From the French by Rev. Fr. Bradbury. 12mo., 1s. 6d.; better bound, 3s. 6d.

Kainer ; or, the Usurer's Doom. By James King. 1s.

KAVANAGH (Rev. P. F.), Insurrection of '98. 2s.

KEENAN (Rev. S.), Controversial Catechism. 12mo., 2s.

Keighley Hall, and other Tales. By E. King. Gilt, 2s.

KENNY (Dr.), Young Catholic's Guide to Confession and Holy Communion. 32mo., 4d.; cloth, 6d.; red edges, 9d. roan, 1s. 6d.; calf or morocco, 2s.

—————— **New Year's Gift to our Heavenly Father.** 4d.

KERSHAW (Frances J. M.), Bobbie and Birdie ; or, Our Lady's Picture. A Story for the very little ones. 2s. 6d.

Key of Heaven. *See* Prayers, page 31.

Killed at Sedan. A Novel. By Samuel Richardson, A.B., B.L. 10s. 6d.

KINANE (Rev. T. H.), Angel of the Altar ; or, the Love of the Most Adorable and Most Sacred Heart of Jesus. 2s. 6d.

—————— **Dove of the Tabernacle.** 1s. 6d.

—————— **Lamb of God.** 18mo., 2s.

—————— **Mary Immaculate.** 2s.

KING (Elizabeth), Keighley Hall, &c., gilt, 2s.
———— The Silver Teapot. 18mo., 4d.
KING (James). Industry and Laziness. 12mo., 3s.
———— Kalner ; or, the Usurer's Doom. 1s.
Kishoge Papers. Tales of Devilry and Drollery. 12mo., 1s. 6d.
Knock ; Apparitions and Miracles. 1s.
———— Three Visits to. 2s.
LA BOUILLERIE (Mgr. de), The Eucharist and the Christian Life. Translated by L. C. 12mo., 3s. 6d.
Lacordaire. The Inner Life of Pere Lacordaire. From the French of Père Chocarne. By Augusta Theodosia Drane. 6s. 6d.
Lady Mildred's Housekeeper, A Few Words from. 2d.
LAIDLAW (Mrs. Stuart), Letters to my God-child. No. 4. On the Veneration of the Blessed Virgin. 16mo., 4d.
LAING (Rev. Dr.), Blessed Virgin's Root traced in the Tribe of Ephraim. 8vo., 10s. 6d.
———— Knight of the Faith. 12mo., 5s.
    Absurd Protestant Opinions concerning *Intention.* 4d.
    Catholic, not Roman Catholic. 4d.
    Challenge to the Churches. 1d.
    Descriptive Guide to the Mass. 1s. and 1s. 6d.
    Favourite Fallacy about Private Judgment and Inquiry. 1d.
    Protestantism against the Natural Moral Law. 1d.
    Shortcomings of the English Catholic Press. 6d.
    What is Christianity? 6d.
    Whence does the Monarch get his right to Rule? 2s. 6d.
LAMBILOTTE (Pere), The Consoler. Translated by Abbot Burder. 12mo., 4s. 6d. ; red edges, 5s.
LANE-CLARKE (T. M. L.) The Violet Sellers. A Drama for Children in 3 Acts. 6d.
LANGUET (Mgr.), Confidence in the Mercy of God. Translated by Abbot Burder. 12mo., 3s.
Last of the Catholic O'Malleys. By M. Taunton. 18mo., 1s. 6d. ; stronger bound, 2s.
Leaflets. 1d. each, or 1s. 2d. per 100 post free, (a single dozen 5d.).
    Act of Reparation to the Sacred Heart.
    Archconfraternity of the Agonising Heart of Jesus and the Compassionate Heart of Mary : Prayers for the Dying.
    Archconfraternity of Our Lady of Angels.
    Ditto, Rules.
    Christmas Offering (or 7s. 6d. per 1000).
    Devotions to S. Joseph.
    Divine Praises.
    Gospel according to S. John, *in Latin.* 1s. 6d. per 100.
    Indulgenced Prayers for Souls in Purgatory.
    Indulgences attached to Medals, Crosses, Statues, &c.
    Intentions for Indulgences.
    Litany of Our Lady of Angels.
    Litany of S. Joseph, and Devotions.
    Litany of Resignation.
    Miraculous Prayer—August Queen of Angels.
    Picture of Crucifixion, "I thirst" (or 5s. per 1000).

R. Washbourne, 18 *Paternoster Row, London.*

Prayer for One's Confessor.
Prayers for the Holy Souls in Purgatory. By St. Ligouri.
Reasonings of Plain Common-Sense upon the Church (2s. 10d.
  per 100, post free).
Union of our Life with the Passion of our Lord.
Visit to the Blessed Sacrament.

Leaflets. 1d. each, or 6s. per 100, (a single dozen 10d., post free).
Act of Consecration to the Sacred Heart.
Concise Portrait of the Blessed Virgin.
Explanation of the Medal or Cross of St. Benedict.
Indulgenced Prayers for the Rosary of the Holy Souls.
Indulgenced Prayer before a Crucifix.
Indulgences, Short Explanation of. By Rev. A. J. Matthews.
Litany of Our Lady of Lourdes.
Litany of the Seven Dolours.
Office of the Sacred Heart.
Prayer to S. Philip Neri.
Prayers before and after Holy Communion.
Reasons showing there must be a true Church.

Lectures for Boys. By Canon Doyle. 2 vols., 12mo., 10s. 6d.
Legends of the Blessed Virgin. 12mo., 3s. 6d.
Legends of the Commandments of God. 12mo., 3s. 6d.
Legends of the Saints. By M. F. S. 16mo., 3s. 6d.
Legends of the Thirteenth Century. By Rev. H. Collins.
  3s., or in 3 vols., 1s. 6d. each.
LEGUAY (Abbe), The Postulant and Novice. 2s. 6d.
Lenten Thoughts. By Bishop Amherst. 18mo., 1s. ; stronger
  bound, 2s., with red edges, 2s. 6d.
Letters to my God-child. By Mrs. Stuart Laidlaw. 16mo., 4d.
Life of Pleasure. By Mgr. Dechamps. 12mo., 1s. 6d.
Light of the Holy Spirit in the World. Five Sermons by
  Bishop Hedley. 12mo., 1s. ; cloth, 1s. 6d.
LIGUORI (S.), Fourteen Stations of the Cross. 18mo., 1d.
———— Selva ; or, a Collection of Matter for Sermons. 12mo., 5s.
———— Way of Salvation. 32mo., 1s.
Lily of S. Joseph : A little Manual of Prayers and Hymns for
  Mass. 64mo., 2d. ; cloth, 3d., 4d., and 6d. ; gilt, 8d. ; roan, 1s.;
  French morocco, 1s. 6d.; calf or morocco, 2s.; gilt, 2s. 6d.
LINGARD (Dr.), Gunpowder Plot. 8vo., 2s. 6d.
———— Anglo-Saxon Church. 2 vols., 12mo., 10s.
Links with the Absent ; or, Chapters on Correspondence. By
  a Member of the Ursuline Community, Thurles. [*In the press.*
Little Mildred, or Oremus. By F. B. Bickerstaffe Drew. 1s.
Little Prayer Book. 32mo., 3d.
**Lives of the First Religious of the Visitation of Holy
  Mary.** By Mother Frances Magdalen de Chaugy. 2 vols., 10s.
Lost Children of Mount St. Bernard. 18mo., 6d.
Lourdes, Our Blessed Lady of. By Rev. Dr. Husenbeth.
  18mo., 6d.; with the Novena, 1s.; cloth, 1s. 6d.
———— Novena of, for the use of the Sick. 4d.
———— Litany of. 1d. each.
———— Month at Lourdes. By H. Caraher. 2s.

LUCK (Dom Edmund J.), Short Meditations for every Day in the Year. From the Italian. 12mo. Edition for the Regular Clergy, 2 vols., 9s.; edn. for the Secular Clergy and others, 2 vols., 9s.

———— S. Gregory's Life and Miracles of St. Benedict. 31s. 6d. ; cheap edition, 10s. 6d. ; small edition, 2s. and 2s. 6d.

LYONS (C. B.), Catholic Choir Manual. 12mo., 1s.

———— Catholic Psalmist. 12mo., 4s.

MACDANIEL (M. A.), Month of May. 18mo., 2s.

———— Novena to S. Joseph. 32mo., 4d.; cloth, 6d.

———— Road to Heaven. A Game. 1s. and 2s.

MACEVILLY (Bishop), Exposition of the Epistles of St. Paul and of the Catholic Epistles. 2 vols., large 8vo. 18s.

———— Exposition of the Gospels. Large 8vo., SS. Matthew, and Mark, 12s. 6d., S. Luke, 6s.

MANAHAN (Dr.), Triumph of the Catholic Church in the Early Ages. 12mo., 5s.

Manning (Card.) A Biographical Sketch ; with some account of Catholicism since 1829. Cloth 1s. 6d., paper 6d.

MANNING (Cardinal): Confraternity of the Holy Family. 3d.

MANNOCK (Patrick), Origin and Progress of Religious Orders, and Happiness of a Religious State. Translated from the Latin of Rev. F. Platus. 12mo., 2s. 6d.

Manual of Catholic Devotions. *See* Prayers, page 31.

Manual of Devotions in honour of Our Lady of Sorrows. Compiled by the Clergy at St. Patrick's, Soho. 18mo., 1s. & 1s. 6d.

Manuel de Conversation. 12mo., 6d.

Map of London, with Alphabetical List of the Catholic Churches, and view of the proposed Westminster Cathedral. 6d.

Margarethe Verflassen. Translated from the German by Mrs. Smith Sligo. 12mo., 1s. 6d. and 3s.; gilt, 3s. 6d.

MARQUIGNY (Pere), Life and Letters of Countess Adelstan. 12mo., 1s. and 2s. 6d.

MARSHALL (A. J. P., Esq.), Comedy of Convocation in the English Church. 8vo., 2s. 6d. *

———— English Religion. 8vo. 6d.,

———— Infallibility of the Pope. 8vo., 1s. *

———— Oxford Undergraduate of Twenty Years Ago. 8vo., 2s. 6d.; cloth, 3s. 6d. *

———— Reply to the Bishop of Ripon's Attack on the Catholic Church. 8vo., 6d. *

———— Two Bibles. A Contrast. 16mo., 1s. 6d.

MARSHALL (T. W. M., Esq.), Harmony of Anglicanism—Church Defence. 8vo., 2s. 6d. *

The 5 (*) *in one Volume, 8vo., Marshallianae,* 6s.

MARSHALL (Rev. W.), The Doctrine of Purgatory. 1s.

———— A Squib for the Saints. 3d.

MARTIN (Rev. E. R.), Rule of the Pope-King. 8vo., 6d.

Mary Immaculate, Devotion to. By Rev. T. H. Kinane. 2s.

Mary, New Month of. By Bishop Kenrick. 32mo., 1s. 6d.

Mary Venerated in all Ages—Regina Sæculorum. 12mo., 3s., cheap edition, 1s.

Mass, Descriptive Guide to. By Rev. Dr. Laing. 12mo., 1s., or stronger bound, 1s. 6d.

Mass, Devotions for. Very *Large type*, 18mo., 3d.

Mass (The). By Müller, 10s. 6d. Tronson, 4d. O'Brien, 9s.

Mass, A Devout Exposition of. By Rev. A. J. Rowley. 4s.

MATIGNON (Pere) The Duties of Christian Parents. 5s.

MAUREL (Rev. F. A.), Indulgences. 18mo., 2s.

Maxims of the Kingdom of Heaven. 12mo., 5s. ; red edges, 5s. 6d. ; calf or mor., 10s. 6d. Old Testament, 1s. 6d. ; Gospels, 1s.

May, Festivals. By Canon Doyle. 12mo., 2s. 6d.

May, Month of. By Rev. P. Comerford. 32mo., 1s.

May, Month of, principally for the use of Religious. 18mo., 1s. 6d.

May Readings for the Feasts of Our Lady. By Rev. A. P. Bethell. 18mo., 1s., stronger bound, 1s. 6d.

May Templeton ; a Tale of Faith and Love. 12mo., 5s.

M'CORRY (Rev. Dr.), Monks of Iona. 8vo., 3s. 6d.

———— Rome, Past, Present, Future. 8vo., 6d.

MCNEILL (Rev. Mark), The Faith. 12mo., 5s.

Meditations for every Day in the Year. By Fr. Luck. 9s.

MEEHAN (M. H.), Fairy Tales for Little Children. 12mo., 6d. and 1s. ; stronger bound, 1s. 6d. ; gilt, 2s.

MERMILLOD (Mgr.), The Supernatural Life. Translated from the French, with a Preface by Lady Herbert. 12mo., 5s.

MEYRICK (Rev. T.), Life of St. Wenefred. 12mo., 2s.

———— Lives of the Early Popes. St. Peter to St. Sylvester. 4s. 6d. From the time of Constantine to Charlemagne. 5s. 6d.

———— St. Eustace. A Drama (5 Acts) for Boys. 12mo., 1s.

M. F. S., Catherine Hamilton. 12mo., 2s. 6d. ; gilt, 3s.

———— Catherine Grown Older. 12mo., 2s. 6d. ; gilt, 3s.

———— Fluffy. A Tale for Boys. 12mo., 3s. 6d.

———— Jack's Boy. 12mo., 3s. 6d.

———— Legends of the Saints. 16mo., 3s. 6d. [gilt, 1s. 6d.

———— My Golden Days. 12mo., 2s. 6d. ; or in 3 vols., 1s. ea.,

———— Our Esther. [*In the press.*

———— Out in the Cold World. 12mo., 3s. 6d.

———— Stories of Holy Lives. 12mo., 3s. 6d.

———— Stories of Martyr Priests. 12mo., 3s. 6d.

———— Stories of the Saints. Five Series, 12mo., 3s. 6d. each.

———————— First and Second Series ; gilt, 4s. 6d. each.

———— Story of the Life of S. Paul. 2s. 6d. and 1s. 6d.

———— The Three Wishes. A Tale. 12mo., 2s. 6d. and 1s. 6d.

———— Tom's Crucifix, and other Tales. 12mo., 3s. 6d., or in 5 vols., 1s. each, gilt, 1s. 6d.

MILNER (Bishop), Devotion to the Sacred Heart of Jesus. 32mo., 3d. ; cloth, 6d. [2d.

Miracle at Rome, through the intercession of B. John Berchmans.

Miraculous Cure of Blindness, through the intercession of Our Lady and S. Ignatius. 12mo., 2d.

Misgivings—Convictions. 12mo., 6d.

Missal. *See* Prayers, page 31.

MOEHLER (Dr.), Symbolism. Translated by Professor Robertson. 12mo., 8s.

Monastic Legends. By E. G. K. Browne. 8vo., 6d.

MOHR (Rev. J., S.J.), Cantiones Sacrae. Hymns and Chants. Music and Words. 8vo., 5s.

—————— **Manual of Sacred Chant.** Music and Words. 2s. 6d.

MOLLOY (Rev. Dr.), Passion Play at Ober-Ammergau. 2s. ; with Photograph, 3s.

Monk of the Monastery of Yuste. By Mariana Monteiro. 2s. 6d.

Monks of Iona and the Duke of Argyll. By M'Corry. 3s. 6d.

MONSABRE (Rev. Pere), Gold and Alloy. 12mo., 2s. 6d.

MONTAGU (Lord Robert), Civilization and the See of Rome. 8vo., 6d.

Montalembert (Count de). By George White. 12mo., 6d.

MONTEIRO (Mariana), Allah Akbar—God is Great. An Arab Legend of the Siege and Conquest of Granada. 12mo., 3s. 6d.

—————— **Monk of the Monastery of Yuste ; or, The Last Days of the Emperor Charles V.** An Historical Legend of the 16th Century. 12mo., 2s. 6d.

—————— **Gathered Gems from Spanish Authors.** 12mo., 3s.

—————— **Sanctuary Meditations.** By Fr. Gracian. 4s.

MOORE'S Irish Melodies. With Symphonies and Accompaniments by John Stevenson and Sir Henry Bishop. 4to., 3s. 6d.

Mora (Ven. Elizabeth Canori), Life of. Translated from the Italian, with Preface by Lady Herbert. With Photograph. 3s. 6d.

MORAN (Rt. Rev. Dr.) Irish Saints in Great Britain. 5s.

MULHOLLAND (Rosa), Prince and Saviour : The Story of Jesus. 12mo., 1s. 6d.; 32mo., 6d. and 2d.

MULLER (Rev. M.), The Holy Mass. 12mo., 10s. 6d.

Multiplication Table, on a sheet. 3s. per 100.

MURRAY-LANE (Chevalier H.), Chronological Sketch of the Kings of England and the Kings of France, 12mo. 2s. 6d.; or in 2 vols., 1s. 6d. each.

MUSIC : Antiphons of the B.V.M. (S. Cecilian). 3s. 6d.

Ave Maria, for Four Voices. By W. Schulthes. 1s. 3d.

Caecilian Society. *See* Separate List.

Catholic Choralist. 12 Numbers for 3s.

Catholic Hymnal. By Leopold de Prins. 2s.; bound, 3s.

Cor Jesu, Salus in Te sperantium. By W. Schulthes, 2s.; with Harp Accompaniment, 2s. 6d.; abridged, 3d.

Corona Lauretana. 20 Litanies by W. Schulthes. 2s.

Evening Hymn at the Oratory. By Rev. J. Nary. 3d.

Litanies (36) and Benediction Service. By W. Schulthes. 6s. Second Series (Corona Lauretana). 2s.

Litanies (6). By E. Leslie. 6d.

Litanies (18). By Rev. J. McCarthy. 1s. 6d.

Litany of the B.V.M. By Baronnesse Emma Freemantle. 6d.

Mass of St. Patrick. For three equal voices. By F. Schaller. 2s. 6d.

Mass of the Holy Child Jesus. In Unison. By W. Schulthes. 3s. The vocal part only, 4d. ; or 3s. per doz. Cloth, 6d. ; or 4s. 6d. per doz.

Missa, Jesu bone Pastor. By Schaller. 3s. 6d.
Moore's Irish Melodies. 4to., 3s. 6d.
Motetts (Five), S. Cecilian Society. 3s. 6d.
Ne projicias me a facie Tua. Motett for Four Voices.
 By W. Schulthes. 1s. 3d.
Oratory Hymns. By W. Schulthes. 2 vols., 8s.
Recordare. Oratorio Jeremiæ Prophetæ. By the same. 1s.
Regina Cœli. Motett for Four Voices. By W. Schul-
 thes. 3s. Vocal Arrangement, 1s.
Six Sacred Vocal Pieces, for three or four equal
 Voices. By W. Schulthes. 4s.
Six Invocations, for four equal Voices. By W.
 Schulthes. 1s. 6d.
Twelve Latin Hymns. By W. Schulthes. 1s. 6d.
Veni Domine. Motett for Four Voices. By W. Schul-
 thes. 2s. Vocal Arrangement, 6d.
Vesper Psalms and Magnificat. By A.W. Hutton. 3s.
 ₊ *All the above (music) prices are nett.*
My Conversion and Vocation. By Rev. Father Schouvaloff, 5s.
My Golden Days. By M. F. S. 12mo., 2s. 6d., or in 3 vols., 1s.
 each ; or 1s. 6d. gilt.
My Lady at Last. A Tale, by M. Taunton. 5s.
NARY (Rev. J.), Evening Hymn at the Oratory. Music, 3d.
Natural Philosophy, Catechism of. 18mo., 3d.
Necessity of Enquiry as to Religion. By H. J. Pye. 6d.
Nellie Gordon, the Factory Girl; or, Lost and Saved. By
 M. A. Pennell. 18mo., 6d.
NEVIN (Willis, Esq.), The Jesuits, and other Essays. 2s. 6d.
NEWMAN (Cardinal), St. Athanasius : Select Treatise
 in Controversy with the Arians. 2 vols., 15s.
New Testament. 12mo., 2s. 6d. Persian calf, 7s. 6d., morocco,
 10s. Illustrated, large 4to., 7s. 6d.
New Year's Gift to Our Heavenly Father. 32mo., 4d.
Nicholas ; or, the Reward of a Good Action. 18mo., 6d.
Nina and Pippo, the Lost Children of Mt. St. Bernard. 6d.
NOETHEN (Rev. T.), Good Thoughts for Priests and
· People ; or, Short Meditations for every Day in the Year. 8s.
———— Compendium of Church History. 12mo., 8s.
NOUET (Rev. J.) Meditations on the Life of Our Lord,
 for every day in the Year. 2 vols. 7s. 6d.
Novena to Our Blessed Lady of Lourdes for the use of
 the Sick. 18mo., 4d.
Novena of Grace, revealed by S. Francis Xavier. 18mo., 6d.
Novena of Meditations in honour of St. Joseph, according to
 the method of St. Ignatius, preceded by a new method of hearing
 Mass according to the intentions of the Souls in Purgatory. 18mo., 1s.
Novena of Meditations. By Sister Mary Alphonsus. 2s. 6d.
Occasional Prayers for Festivals. *See* Prayers, page 31.
O'CLERY (Keyes, K.S.G.), The History of the Italian
 Revolution. First Period—The Revolution of the Barricades
 (1796-1849). 8vo., 7s. 6d. Cheap edition 3s. 6d.

O'GALLAGHER (Dr.), Sermons in Irish-Gaelic; with literal idiomatic English Translation. By Canon U. J. Bourke. 7s. 6d.

O'HARA (C. M.), Clare's Sacrifice. An impressive little Tale for First Communicants. 6d.

O'KEEFE (Rev. P.) Moral Discourses. 18mo., 2s.

O'MAHONY (D.P.M.), Rome semper eadem. 8vo., 1s. 6d.

O'MEARA (Kathleen), The Battle of Connemara. 12mo., 3s.

———— A Daughter of S. Dominick (Bells of the Sanctuary, No. 4). 12mo., 1s.; stronger bound, 1s. 6d. and 2s.

On what Authority do I accept Christianity? 12mo., 6d.

Op BROEK (Rev. A.), Search the Scriptures. 7s. 6d.

Oratorian Lives of the Saints. With Portrait, 12mo., 5s. a vol.
    I. S. Bernardine of Siena, Minor Observatine.
    II. S. Philip Benizi, Fifth General of the Servites.
    III. S. Veronica Giuliani, and B. Battista Varani.
    IV. S. John of God. By Canon Cianfogni.

O'REILLY (Rev. Dr.), Victims of the Mamertine. 5s.

————A Romance of Repentance. 12mo., 3s. 6d.

Oremus; or, Little Mildred. By Rev. F. Drew. 1s.

Oremus, A Liturgical Prayer Book. *See* page 31.

Our Esther. By M. F. S., author of "Out in the Cold World." *[In the press.*

Our Lady (Devotion to) in N. America. By Fr. Macleod. 7s. 6d.

Our Lady's Festivals. By Canon Doyle. 2s. 6d.

Our Lady's Lament. By C. E. Tame. 2s.

Our Lady's Month. By Rev. A. P. Bethell. 18mo., 1s. and 1s. 6d

Our Lord's Life, Passion, Death, and Resurrection. 1s.

———— By Rev. H. Rutter. Illustrated. 12mo., 5s.

———— Incidents. A Series of 12 Illuminations. 4to., 6s.

Out in the Cold World. By M. F. S., Author of "Fluffy." 3s. 6d.

OXENHAM (H. N.), Poems. 12mo., 3s. 6d.

Oxford Undergraduate of Twenty Years Ago. By a Bachelor of Arts. 8vo., 2s. 6d.; cloth, 3s. 6d.

OZANAM (A. F.), Protestantism and Liberty. Translated from the French by Wilfrid C. Robinson. 8vo., 1s.

PAGANI (Rev. J. B.), Science of the Saints. 4 vols., 12mo., 15s.

Panegyrics of Fr. Segneri, S.J. Translated from the original Italian. With a Preface, by Rev. W. Humphrey, S.J., 12mo., 6s.

Paradise of God; or the Virtues of the Sacred Heart. By Author of "God our Father," "Happiness of Heaven." 12mo., 4s.

Paray le Monial, and Bl. Margaret Mary. 18mo., 6d.

Passion of Our Lord. Lectures by Canon Doyle. 3s.

Passion of Our Lord, Harmony of. By Gayrard, 1s. 6d. Walsh, 2s.

PASSIONIST FATHERS: Christian Armed. 1s. 6d.
    Sacred Eloquence. 18mo., 2s.
    S. Joseph's Manual of a Happy Eternity. 2s. 6d.
    S. Paul of the Cross. 12mo., 3s.
    School of Jesus Crucified. 18mo., 2s. 6d.

Pater Noster; or, an Orphan Boy. By Rev. F. Drew 1s.

Path to Paradise. *See* Prayers, page 31.

Patrick (S.), Life of. 1s.; 8vo., 6s.; gilt, 10s.

Penitential Psalms. By Rev. F. Blyth. 1s. 6d.

PENNELL (M. A.), Bertram Eldon. 12mo., 1s.
———— Agnes Wilmott's History, and the Lessons it Taught. 1s. 6d.
———— Nellie Gordon, the Factory Girl. 18mo., 6d.
Pens, Washbourne's Free and Easy. Fine, or Middle, or Broad Points, 1s. per gross.
Perpetual Adoration, Book of. By Boudon. 3s. and 3s. 6d.
Per Jesum Christum ; or, Two Good Fridays. By Rev. F. Drew. 1s.
Peter (S.), his Name and his Office. By T. W. Allies. 5s.
Peter, Years of. By an ex-Papal Zouave. 12mo., 1d.
Philip Benizi (S.), Life of. 5s.
Philosophy, Elements of. By Rev. W. H. Hill. 8vo., 6s.
PHILPIN (Rev. F.), Holy Places; their sanctity and authenticity. With three Maps. 12mo., 2s. 6d. and 6s.
Photographs (10) illustrating the History of the Miraculous Hosts. (Cathedral, Brussels.) 2s. 6d. the set.
PILLEY (C.), Walter Ferrers' School Days ; or, Bellevue and its Owners. 12mo., 2s.
Pius IX., from his Birth to his Death. By G. White. 4d.
Plain Chant. The Cecilian Society Music kept in stock.
PLATUS (Rev. F.), Origin and Progress of Religious Orders, and Happiness of a Religious State. 12mo., 2s. 6d.
PLAYS. *See* Dramas, page 10.
PLUES (Margaret), Chats about the Commandments. 3s.
———— Chats about the Rosary. 3s.
POOR CLARES OF KENMARE. *See* Cusack (Miss).
Pope-King, Rule of. By Rev. E. R. Martin. 8vo., 6d.
Popes of Rome. By Rev. C. Tondini. 3s. 6d.
Popes, Lives of the Early. By Rev. T. Meyrick. 2 vols. 10s.'
Portiuncula, Indulgence of. 3d. ; 12 for 2s. ; 150 for 20s.
POTTER (Rev. T. J.), Extemporary Preaching. 2s. 6d.
———— Farleyes of Farleye. 12mo., 2s. 6d.
———— Pastor and People. 12mo., 5s.
———— Percy Grange. 12mo., 3s.
———— Rupert Aubrey. 12mo., 3s.
———— Sir Humphrey's Trial. 12mo., 2s. 6d.
POWELL (J., Esq.), Two Years in the Pontifical Zouaves. Illustrated. 8vo., 3s. 6d.
POWER (Rev. P.) Catechism. 3 vols., 10s. 6d. ; 2 vols. 7s. 6d.
PRADEL (Fr., O. P.), Life of St. Vincent Ferrer. Translated by Rev. Fr. Dixon. With a Photograph. 12mo., 5s.
PRAYER BOOKS. *See* page 31.
PRICE (Rev. E.), Sick Calls. 12mo., 3s. 6d.
PRINS (Leopold de). *See* Music.
Pro-Cathedral, Kensington. Tinted View of the Interior ; 11 × 15 inches, 1s.; Proofs, on larger paper, 2s.
PROCTOR (John), A Lay Convert on the Catholic Church. Three Lectures. 12mo., cloth, 1s.
Prophecies, Contemporary. By Mgr. Dupanloup. 8vo., 1s.
Protestantism and Liberty. By F. Ozanam. 1s
Protestant Principles examined by the Written Word. 1s.
· Prussian Spy. A Novel. By V. Valmont. 12mo., 4s.

R. Washbourne, 18 *Paternoster Row, London.*

Purgatory, Month of the Souls in Purgatory. By Ricard, 1s.
Purgatory, The Doctrine of. By Rev. W. Marshall. 12mo., 1s.
Purgatory, Souls in. By Abbot Burder. 32mo., 3d.
PYE (Henry John, M.A.), Necessity of Enquiry as to
  Religion. 32mo., 4d.; cloth, 6d.
———— Revelation. Being the substance of several conversations
  on First Principles. 6d.
———— The Religion of Common Sense. New Edition. 1s.
RAVIGNAN (Pere), The Spiritual Life, Conferences.
  Translated by Mrs. Abel Ram. 12mo., 5s.
Ravignan (Pere), Life of. 12mo., 12s.
RAYMOND-BARKER (Mrs. F.) Life of Countess Adel-
  stan. 1s. and 2s. 6d.
———— Fr. Hermann (Carmelite). 5s. 6d. and 6s. 6d.
———— Paul Seigneret. 12mo., 6d., 1s., 1s. 6d., gilt, 2s.
———— Regina Sæculorum. 12mo., 1s. and 3s.
———— Rosalie. 12mo., 1s., 1s. 6d., gilt, 2s.
Reading Books, by the Marist Brothers. 12mo., 1st, 4d.; 2nd, 7d.
Reasonings of Plain Common-Sense upon the Church.
  2s. 10d. a 100, post free.
REDMAN (Rev. Dr.), Book of Perpetual Adoration. By
  Mgr. Boudon. 12mo., 3s.; red edges, 3s. 6d.
REDMOND (Rev. Dr.), Sermon Essays. 18mo., 1s.
REEVES' History of the Bible. 12mo., 3s. 6d. 18mo., 1s.
Reflections, One Hundred Pious. By Alban Butler. 1s.
Regina Sæculorum; or, Mary Venerated in all Ages. Devotions
  to the Blessed Virgin from Ancient Sources. 12mo., 1s. and 3s.
Rejection of Catholic Doctrines attributable to the Non-
  Realization of Primary Truths. 8vo., 1s.
Religion of Common Sense. By H. J. Pye, M.A. 12mo., 1s.
Religious Orders. By Rev. F. Platus. 2s. 6d.
Rest, on the Cross. By Eleanora Louisa Hervey. 12mo., 3s. 6d.
Revelation. By Henry John Pye, Esq. 6d.
Reverse of the Medal. A Drama for Girls. 12mo., 6d.
RIBADENEIRA—Life of Our Lord. 12mo., 1s.
RICARD (Abbe), Month of the Holy Angels. 18mo., 1s.
———— Month of the Souls in Purgatory. 18mo., 1s.
RICE (Rev. F. S.), Lina : an Italy Lily. 16mo., 1s. 6d.
RICHARDSON (Rev. Fr.), Catholic Sick and Benefit
  Club; or, the Guild of our Lady; and St. Joseph's Catholic
  Burial Society. 32mo., 4d.
———— Holy War against Drunkenness. Manual 6d. a
  dozen, Cards 2d. each.
———— Little by Little; or, the Penny Bank. 32mo., 1d.
———— Shamrocks. 6s. 2d. a gross (144), post free.
———— S. Joseph's Catholic Burial Society. 2d.
———— The Crusade. For the Suppression of Drunkenness. 1d.
RICHARDSON (Samuel, A.B., B.L., of the Middle
  Temple), Killed at Sedan. A Novel. Crown 8vo., 7s. 6d.
Ritus Servandus in Expositione et Benedictione. Red cloth,
  7s. 6d., red morocco, 10s.
Road to Heaven. A Game. By Miss M. A. Macdaniel. 1s. and 2s.
ROBERTSON (Professor), Edmund Burke. 12mo., 3s. 6d.

ROBINSON (Wilfrid C.), Protestantism and Liberty. Translated from the French of Professor Ozanam. 8vo., 1s.

Roman Question, The. By Rev. Dr. Husenbeth. 8vo., 6d.

Rome and her Captors : Letters collected and edited by Count Henri d'Ideville, and Translated by F. R. Wegg-Prosser. 4s.

Rome, Past, Present, and Future. By Dr. M'Corry. 8vo., 6d.

―――― Personal Recollections of. By W. J. Jacob, 8vo., 6d.

―――― The Victories of. By Rev. F. Beste. 8vo., 1s.

―――― (To) and Back. Fly-Leaves from a Flying Tour. Edited by Rev. W. H. Anderdon, S.J., 12mo., 2s.

Rosalie ; or, the Memoir of a French Child, told by herself. By Mrs. F. Raymond-Barker. 1s.; stronger bound, 1s. 6d.; gilt, 2s.

Rosary, Fifteen Mysteries of, and Fourteen Stations of the Cross. In One Volume, 32 Illustrations. 16mo., 2s.

Rosary for the Souls in Purgatory, with Indulgenced Prayer. 6d. and 9d. Medals separately, 1d. each, or 9s. gross. Prayers separately, 1d. each, 9d. a dozen, or 6s. for 100.

Rosary, Chats about the; Aunt Margaret's Little Neighbours. 3s.

Rose of Venice. A Tale. By S. Christopher. Crown 8vo., 5s.

ROWLEY (Rev. Austin John), A Devout Exposition of the Holy Mass. Composed by John Heigham. 12mo., 4s.

RUSSELL (Rev. M.), Emmanuel. 2s. ; cheap edition, 6d.

―――― Madonna. Verses on Our Lady and the Saints, 2s.

RUTTER (Rev. H.) Life and Sufferings of Our Lord, with Introduction by Rev. Dr. Husenbeth. Illustrated. 12mo., 5s.

RYAN (Bishop). What Catholics do not Believe. 12mo., 1s.

Sacred Heart. Act of Consecration to. 1d.; or 6s. per 100.

―――――――, Act of Reparation to. 1s. 2d. per 100.

―――――――, A Novena. 1s.

―――――――, A Spiritual Bouquet. 6d.; cloth gilt, 1s.

―――――――, Devotions to. By Rev. S. Franco. 12mo., 4s.

―――――――, Devotions to. By Bishop Milner. 3d.; cloth, 6d.

―――――――, Elevations to the. By Rev. Fr. Doyotte, S.J. 3s.

―――――――, Golden Treasury. 48mo., 1s. 6d.; French morocco, 2s. 6d. ; calf or morocco, 3s. 6d.

―――――――, The Heart of Jesus at Nazareth. 3s. 6d.

―――――――, Hours with. 2s.

―――――――, Lectures. By Canon Doyle. 3s.

―――――――, Letters of Blessed Margaret Mary. 3s.

―――――――, Little Treasury of. 32mo., 2s.; French morocco, 2s. 6d.; calf, 5s. ; morocco, 6s.

―――――――― offered to the Piety of the Young engaged in Study. By Rev. F. Deham. 32mo., 9d.

―――――――, Office. 1d.

―――――――― *See* Paradise of God, 4s. ; Kinane (Rev. T. H.), 2s. 6d.

―――――――, Pearls from the Casquet. 3s.

―――――――, Pleadings of. By Rev. M. Comerford. 18mo., 1s.

―――――――, Treasury of. 32mo., 2s.; French morocco, 2s. 6d.; calf, 5s.; morocco, 6s. 18mo., 3s. 6d.; roan, 4s.

Sacred History in Forty Pictures. Plain, 5s.; coloured, 7s, 6d. mounted on cardboard, coloured, 18s. 6d. and 22s.

Saints, Lives of, for every day in the Year. Beautifully printed, within illustrated borders from ancient sources, on thick toned paper. 4to., gilt, 25s. *Only a few copies left.*

ST. JURE (S.J.) Knowledge and Love of Jesus Christ. 3 vols., 8vo., 31s. 6d.

———— **The Spiritual Man.** 12mo., 6s.

Sanctuary Meditations for Priests and Frequent Communicants. Translated from the Spanish of Fr. Baltasar Gracian, by Mariana Monteiro. 12mo., 4s.

SCARAMELLI—Directorium Asceticum ; or, Guide to the Spiritual Life. 4 vols. 12mo., 24s.

SCHMID (Canon), Tales. Illustrated. 12mo., 3s. 6d. Separately :—The Canary Bird, The Dove, The Inundation, The Rose Tree, The Water Jug, The Wooden Cross. 6d. each ; gilt, 1s.

Schools supplied with all School Books. 3d. taken off the 1s.

School of Jesus Crucified. By the Passionist Fathers. 18mo., 2s. 6d.

SCHOUVALOFF (Rev. Father, Barnabite), My Conversion and Vocation. Translated from the French, with an Appendix, by Fr. C. Tondini. 12mo., 5s.

SCHULTHES (William). *See* Music.

SEAMER (Mrs.), *See* M. F. S., page 19.

SEGNERI (Fr., S.J.), Panegyrics. Translated from the original Italian. With a Preface, by Rev. W. Humphrey. 12mo., 6s.

SEGUR (Mgr.), Books for Little Children. Translated. 32mo., 3d. each. Confession, Holy Communion, Child Jesus, Piety, Prayer, Temptation and Sin. In one volume, cloth, 2s.

———— **Three Roses of the Elect.** 16mo., 1s. 6d.

SEGUR (Countess de), The Little Hunchback. 12mo., 3s.

Seigneret, Seminarist (Paul), Life of. 6d., 1s., and 1s. 6d. ; gilt, 2s.

Selva ; a Collection of Matter for Sermons. By St. Liguori. 12mo., 5s.

Semi-Tropical Trifles. By H. Compton. 12mo., 1s. ; cloth, 2s. 6d.

Sermon Essays. By Rev. Dr. Redmond. 12mo., 1s.

Sermons. Irish and English. By Dr. O'Gallagher. 8vo., 7s. 6d.

———— *See* Doyle, 2 vols., 10s. 6d. ; Scaramelli, 4 vols., 24s. ; Segneri, 6s. ; O'Keeffe, 2s. ; Buckley, 6s.

———— By Rev. J. Perry. First Series, 3s. 6d. Second Series, 3s. 6d.

———— and Instructions, Programmes of. 2 vols., 12s.

———— **The Light of the Holy Spirit in the World.** By Bishop Hedley. 1s. ; cloth, 1s. 6d.

Serving Boy's Manual, and Book of Public Devotions, Containing all those prayers and devotions for Sundays and Holydays, usually divided in their recitation between the Priest and the Congregation. Compiled from approved sources, and adapted to Churches, served either by the Secular or Regular Clergy. 32mo., embossed, 1s. ; French morocco, 2s. ; calf, 4s. ; with Epistles and Gospels, 6d. extra.

SHAKESPEARE. Tragedies and Comedies. Expurgated edition. By Rosa Baughan. 8vo., 6s. The Comedies only, 3s. 6d.

Shandy Maguire. A Farce for Boys. 2 Acts. 12mo., 2s.

SHAW (T. H.), Holy Church the Centre of Unity ; or, Ritualism compared with Catholicism. 8vo., 1s.

———— **The McPhersons,** to which is added "England's Glory ; the Roll of Honour." 8vo., 2s. 6d.

SIGHART (Dr.) Albertus Magnus. 10s. 6d. Cheap edition, 5s.
Silver Teapot. By Elizabeth King. 18mo., 4d.
Simple Tales—Waiting for Father, &c., &c. 16mo., 2s. 6d.
Sir Ælfric and other Tales. By Rev. G. Bampfield. 1s.
Sir Thomas Maxwell and his Ward. By Miss Bridges. 1s.
Sisters of Charity, Manual of. 18mo. 6s.
SMITH–SLIGO (A. V., Esq.), Life of the Ven. Anna Maria
  Taigi. Translated from French of Calixte. 8vo., 2s. 6d. and 5s.
— (Mrs.) **Margarethe Verflassen.** 12mo., 1s. 6d., 3s., and 3s. 6d.
Solid Virtue. By Father Bellécius, S.J. With a Preface by Dr.
  Croke, Archbishop of Cashel and Emly. New edition, revised and
  corrected. Crown 8vo., 7s. 6d.
Sophia and Eulalie. (The Catholic Pilgrim's Progress.) From the
  French by Rev. Fr. Bradbury. 12mo., 1s. 6d., better bound, 3s. 6d.
Spalding (Archbishop), Life of. 8vo., 10s. 6d.
——— Sermon at the Month's Mind. 8vo., 1s.
Spiritual Conferences on the Mysteries of Faith and the
  Interior Life. By Father Collins. 12mo., 5s.
Spiritual Life. Conferences by Père Ravignan. Translated by
  Mrs. Abel Ram. 12mo., 5s.
Spiritual Life of Fr. Schouvaloff. 12mo., 5s.
Spiritual Works of Louis of Blois. Edited by Rev. F. John
  Bowden. 12mo., 3s. 6d.; red edges, 4s.
Stations of the Cross, Method of Blessing, &c. By F.
  Alexis Bulens, O.S.F. 1s. 6d. ; red edges, 2s.
Stations of the Cross, Devotions for Public and Private
  Use at the. By Miss Cusack. Illustrated. 16mo., 1s. and 1s. 6d.
Stations of the Cross. By S. Liguori. 18mo., 1d.
Stations, and Mysteries of the Rosary. Illustrated, 2s.
STEWART (A. M.) St. Angela's Manual. 2s. ; calf, 3s. 6d.
——— Biographical Readings. 12mo., 3s.
——— Cardinal Wolsey. 12mo., 6s. 6d.
——— Sir Thomas More. Illustrated, 10s. 6d.; gilt, 11s. 6d.
——— Life of S. Angela Merici. 12mo., 3s.
——— Life of Bishop Fisher. 12mo., 7s. 6d.
——— Life in the Cloister. 12mo., 3s. 6d.
——— Life of Cardinal Pole. 8s. 6d. ; gilt, 10s. 6d.
——— Limerick Veteran ; or, the Foster Sisters. 5s. and 6s.
——— Margaret Roper. 6s.
——— Yorkshire Plot. 1s. 6d. [1s. ; gilt edges, 1s. 6d.
Stories for my Children—The Angels and the Sacraments.
Stories of Holy Lives. By M. F. S. 12mo., 3s. 6d.
Stories of Martyr Priests. By M. F. S. 12mo., 3s. 6d.
Stories of the Saints. By M. F. S. 12mo., Five Series, each
  3s. 6d. ; 1st and 2nd Series, gilt, 4s. 6d.
Stories from many Lands. Compiled by E. L. Hervey. 3s. 6d.
Story of a Paper Knife. 12mo., 1s. ; gilt edges, 1s. 6d.
Story of Marie and other Tales. 12mo., 2s. 6d.; gilt, 3s.
Story of the Life of St. Paul. By M. F. S., author of "Stories
  of the Saints." 12mo., 2s. 6d., cheap edition, 1s. 6d.
Sufferings of our Lord. Sermons preached by Father Claude de
  la Colombière, S.J., in the Chapel Royal, St. James's, in the year
  1677. 18mo., 1s.; stronger bound, 1s. 6d.; red edges, 2s.

Supernatural Life, The. By Mgr. Mermillod. Translated from the French, with a Preface by Lady Herbert. 12mo., 5s.

Supremacy of the Roman See. By C. E. Tame, Esq. 8vo., 6d.

Sure Way to Heaven. A Little Manual for Confession and Holy Communion. 32mo., 6d.; persian, 2s. 6d.; calf or morocco, 3s. 6d.

Taigi (Anna Maria), Life of. Translated from the French of Calixte by A. V. Smith-Sligo, Esq. 8vo., 2s. 6d. and 5s.

Tales and Sketches. By Charles Fleet. 3s. 6d.

Tales of the Jewish Church. By Charles Walker. 12mo., 2s. 6d., cheap edition, 1s. 6d.

TAME (C. E., Esq.), Early English Literature. 16mo., 2s. a vol. I. Our Lady's Lament, and the Lamentation of S. Mary Magdalene. II. Life of Our Lady, in verse.

—————— **Supremacy of the Roman See.** 8vo., 6d.

TANDY (Rev. Dr.), Terry O'Flinn. 12mo., 1s.; stronger bound, 1s. 6d.; gilt, 2s.   [1s. 6d.; stronger bound, 2s.

TAUNTON (M.), Last of the Catholic O'Malleys. 18mo.,

—————— **My Lady at Last.** A Tale. 5s.

—————— **One Hundred Pious Reflections,** from Alban Butler's Lives of the Saints. 18mo., 1s.; stronger bound, 2s.

TEELING (Mrs. Bartle), The Mission Cross. 2s.; cheap edition, in paper covers, 50 copies for 40s.

TERESA (S.), Book of the Foundations. Translated by Canon Dalton. 12mo., 3s. 6d.

—————— **Letters of.** Translated by Canon Dalton. 12mo., 3s. 6d.

—————— **Way of Perfection.** 12mo., 3s. 6d.

—————— **The Interior Castle.** 12mo., 3s. 6d.

Terry O'Flinn. By Rev. Dr. Tandy. 12mo., 1s., 1s. 6d. and 2s.

Testimony; or, the Necessity of Enquiry as to Religion. By John Henry Pye, M.A. 32mo., 4d.; cloth, 6d.

Theobald; or, The Triumph of Charity. 12mo., 2s. 6d.

Three Wishes. A Tale. By M. F. S. 2s. 6d., cheap edition, 1s. 6d.

Threshold of the Catholic Church. By Fr. Bagshawe. 4s.

Tim O'Halloran's Choice. By Miss Cusack. 3s. 6d.

Tom's Crucifix, and other Tales. By M. F. S. 12mo., 3s. 6d., or in 5 vols., 1s. each; gilt, 1s. 6d.

TONDINI (Rev. Cæsarius), My Conversion and Vocation. By Rev. Fr. Schouvaloff. 12mo., 5s.

—————— **The Pope of Rome and the Popes of the Oriental Orthodox Church.** An essay on Monarchy in the Church, with special reference to Russia. Second Edition. 12mo., 3s. 6d.

—————— **Association Prayers in Honour of Mary Immaculate.** 12mo., 3d.

Transubstantiation, Catholic Doctrine of. 12mo., 6d.

TRONSON (Abbe), The Mass: a devout Method. 32mo., 4d.

TRONSON'S Conferences for Ecclesiastical Students and Religious. By Sister M. F. Clare. 12mo., 4s. 6d.

True Wayside Tales. By Lady Herbert. 12mo., 3s., or cheap edition, in 5 vols., 6d. each.

—————— **Second Series.**   [*In the press.*

Two Friends; or Marie's Self-Denial. By Madame d'Arras. 1s., or

Ursuline Manual. *See* Prayers, page 32.   [gilt, 1s. 6d.

VALMONT (V.), The Prussian Spy. A Novel. 12mo., 4s.

Vatican and the Quirinal. By A. Wood. 1s. 6d.

VAUGHAN (Bishop of Salford), The Mass. 2d.; cloth, 6d.

—————— **Love and Passion of Jesus Christ.** 2d.

Veni Creator; or, Ulrich's Money. By Rev. F. Drew. 1s.

VERE (Rev. G. L.), The Catholic Hymn Book. 32mo., 2d.; cloth, 4d. ; abridged edition, 1d., cloth, 2d.

—————— **For Better, not for Worse.** A Tale. [*In the press.*

Veronica Giuliani (S.), Life of, and B. Battista Varani. With a Photographic Portrait. 12mo., 5s.

Village Lily. A Tale. 12mo., 1s.; gilt, 1s. 6d.

Vincent Ferrer (S.), of the Order of Friar Preachers ; his Life, Spiritual Teaching, and Practical Devotion. By Rev. Fr. Andrew Pradel, O. P. Translated from the French by the Rev. Fr. T. A. Dixon, O.P., with a Photograph. 12mo., 5s.

VINCENT OF LERINS (S.). Commonitory. 12mo., 1s. 3d.

Violet Sellers, The ; a Drama in 3 Acts, for Children. 12mo., 6d.

VIRGIL. Literally translated by Davidson. 12mo., 2s. 6d.

" Vitis Mystica " ; or, the True Vine. By Canon Brownlow. 4s.

WALKER (Charles), Are you Safe in the Church of England ? 8vo., 6d.

—————— **Tales of the Jewish Church.** 12mo., 2s. 6d. and 1s. 6d.

WALLER (J. F., Esq.), Festival Tales. 12mo., 3s. 6d.

Walter Ferrers' School Days; or, Bellevue and its Owners. By C. Pilley. 2s.; cheap edition, 1s.

Weedall (Mgr.), Life of. By Rev. Dr. Husenbeth. 8vo., 5s.

WEGG-PROSSER (F. R.), Rome and her Captors. 4s.

WELD (Miss K. M.), Bessy ; or, the Fatal Consequences of Telling Lies. 1s. ; stronger bound, 1s. 6d. ; gilt, 2s.

Wenefred (St.), Life of. By Rev. T. Meyrick. 12mo., 2s.

WENHAM (Canon), The School Manager. 4s. 6d.

—————— **The Catechumen.** 3s. 6d.

What Catholics do not Believe. By Bishop Ryan. 12mo., 1s.

WHITE (George), Cardinal Wiseman. 12mo., 1s. and 1s. 6d.

—————— **Comte de Montalembert.** 12mo., 6d.

—————— **Life of S. Edmund of Canterbury.** 1s. and 1s. 6d.

—————— **Pius IX., from his Birth to his Death.** 12mo., 4d.

—————— **Queens and Princesses of France.** 12mo., 3s. 6d.

William (St.), of York. A Drama in Two Acts. (Boys.) 12mo., 6d.

WILLIAMS (Canon), Anglican Orders. 12mo., 3s. 6d.

WISEMAN (Cardinal), Doctrines and Practices of the Catholic Church. 12mo., 3s. 6d.

—————— **Science and Religion.** 12mo., 5s.

Wiseman (Cardinal), Life and Obsequies. 1s., cloth, 1s. 6d.

—————— **Recollections of.** By M. J. Arnold. 12mo., 2s. 6d.

WOOD (Alexander), The Vatican and the Quirinal. 1s. 6d.

WOODS (Canon), Defence of the Roman Church against F. Gratry. Translated from the French of Gueranger. 1s.

Young Catholic's Guide to Confession and Holy Communion. By Dr. Kenny. 32mo., 4d.; cloth, 6d.; red edges, 9d., French morocco, 1s. 6d.; calf or morocco, 2s. 6d.

Zouaves Pontifical, Two Years in. By Joseph Powell, Z.P, Illustrated. 8vo., 3s. 6d.

Garden, Little, of the Soul. Edited by the Rev. R. G. Davis. *With Imprimatur of the Cardinal Archbishop of Westminster.* This book, as its name imports, contains a selection from the "Garden of the Soul" of the Prayers and Devotions of most general use. Whilst it will serve as a *Pocket Prayer Book* for all, it is, by its low price, *par excellence*, the Prayer Book for children and for the very poor. In it are to be found the old familiar Devotions of the "Garden of the Soul," as well as many important additions, such as the Devotions to the Sacred Heart, to Saint Joseph, to the Guardian Angels, and others. The omissions are mainly the Forms of administering the Sacraments, and Devotions that are not of very general use. It is printed in a clear type, on a good paper, both especially selected, for the purpose of obviating the disagreeableness of small type and inferior paper. Twentieth Thousand.

    32mo., price, cloth, 6d.; with Epistles and Gospels, 6d.; stronger bound, 8d.; with clasp, 1s.; blue cloth, 1s.; with clasp, 1s.6d. Roan, 1s.; with E. and G. 1s. 6d.; with rims and clasp, 1s. 6d. and 2s. French morocco, 1s. 6d.; with E. and G., 2s.; with rims and clasp, 2s. and 2s. 6d. French morocco extra gilt, 2s.; with E. and G., 2s. 6d.; with rims and clasp, 2s. 6d. and 3s. Calf or morocco, 3s.; with E. and G., 3s. 6d.; with clasp, 4s. and 4s. 6d. Calf or morocco, extra gilt, 4s.; with E. and G., 4s, 6d.; with clasp, 5s. and 5s. 6d. Morocco antique, 7s. 6d., 10s. 6d., 12s., 16s. Velvet, rims and clasp, 5s., 8s. 6d., and 10s. 6d. Russia, 5s., 5s. 6d., 6s., 6s. 6d., 7s. 6d., 8s. Russia antique, 17s. 6d. Ivory, with rims and clasp, 10s. 6d., 13s., 15s., 17s. 6d. Imitation ivory, with rims and clasp, 2s. 6d. Calf or morocco tuck (as a pocket book), 5s. 6d. With oxydized silver or gilt mountings, in morocco case, 25s.

   Illustrated edition, cloth, 1s.; with clasp, 1s. 6d.; roan, 1s. 6d.; French mor., 2s.; extra gilt, 2s. 6d.; calf or morocco, 3s. 6d.; extra gilt, 4s. 6d.

Catholic Piety ; or, Key of Heaven, with Epistles and Gospels. Large 32mo., roan, 1s. 6d. and 2s.; French morocco, with rims and clasp, 2s. 6d.; extra gilt, 3s.; with rims and clasp, 3s. 6d.

Catholic Piety. 32mo., 6d.; rims and clasp, 1s.; French morocco, 1s.; velvet, with rims and clasp, 2s. 6d. With Epistles and Gospels, roan, 1s.; French morocco, 1s. 6d.; with rims and clasp, 2s.; extra gilt, 2s.; Persian, 2s. 6d.; morocco, 3s. 6d.

Key of Heaven, same prices as above.

Crown of Jesus. 18mo., Persian calf, 6s. Calf or Morocco, 8s.; with rims and clasp, 10s. 6d. Calf or morocco, extra gilt, 10s. 6d.; with rims and clasp, 12s. 6d; morocco, with turn-over edges, 10s. 6d. Ivory, with rims and clasp, 21s., 25s., 27s. 6d. and 30s.

Devotions for Mass. Very large type, 12mo., 3d.

Garden of the Soul. Very large Type. 18mo., cloth, 1s.; with Epistles and Gospels, 1s. 6d.; French morocco, 2s. 6d.; with E. and G., 3s. 6d. Best edition, without E. and G., 3s. 6d.; with E. and G., morocco circuit, 7s. 6d.; calf antique, with clasp, 8s. French morocco, antique, with clasp, 6s. 6d.

   Epistles and Gospels, in French morocco, 2s.

Holy Childhood. 6d., 1s. and 1s. 6d.

R. Washbourne, 18 *Paternoster Row, London.*

Child's Picture Prayer Book. 16 tinted Illustrations. Cloth, 1s. and 1s. 6d.; with coloured Illustrations, 1s. 6d., 2s., 2s. 6d., 3s., and 3s. 6d. Roan, 3s. 6d. and 4s. Calf, 5s. and 6s.

Holy Week Book. New edition, with Ordinary of the Mass, Vespers and Complin, Blessing of the Holy Oils, &c. 1s.

Key of Heaven. *Very large type.* 18mo., 1s.; leather, 2s. 6d.

Lily of St. Joseph, The; a little Manual of Prayers and Hymns for Mass. 64mo., price 2d.; cloth, 3d., 4d., 6d., or 8d.; roan, 1s.; French morocco, 1s. 6d.; calf or morocco, 2s.; gilt, 2s. 6d.

Little Prayer Book, The, for Ordinary Catholic Devotions. 3d.

Manual of Catholic Devotions. Small, for the waistcoat pocket. 64mo., 4d.; with Epistles and Gospels, cloth, 6d.; with rims, 1s.; roan, 1s.; calf or morocco, 2s. 6d.; ivorine, 2s. 6d.

Manual of Devotions in Honour of our Lady of Sorrows. 18mo., 1s.; cheaper binding, 1s.

Missal (Complete). 18mo., roan, 5s.; Persian, 7s. 6d.; calf or morocco, 10s. 6d.; with rims and clasp, 13s. 6d.; calf or mor., extra gilt, 12s. 6d., with rims and clasp, 15s. 6d.; morocco, with turn-over edges, 13s. 6d.; morocco antique, 15s.; velvet, 20s.; Russia, 20s.; ivory, with rims and clasp, 31s. 6d. and 35s. A very beautiful edition, handsomely bound in morocco, gilt mountings, silk linings, edges red on gold, in a morocco case. Illustrated, £5.

Missal. Pocket edition. Roan, gilt edges, 2s.

Missal and Vesper Book, in one vol. morocco, 6s.; with clasp, 8s.

Occasional Prayers for Festivals. 4d. and 6d.; gilt, 1s.

Ordinary of the Mass. 32mo., 2d.; cloth, 6d.

Oremus, A Liturgical Prayer Book : with the Imprimatur of the Cardinal Archbishop of Westminster. An adaptation of the Church Offices : containing Morning and Evening Devotions ; Devotion for Mass, Confession, and Communion, and various other Devotions ; Common and Proper, Hymns, Lessons, Collects, Epistles and Gospels for Sundays, Feasts, and Week Days ; and short notices of over 200 Saints' Days. 32mo., 452 pages, 2s. ; cloth, 2s. 6d.; red edges, 3s.; embossed, 3s. 6d.; French morocco, 4s. 6d.; calf or morocco, 6s.; Russia, 8s. 6d., &c., &c., &c.

A Smaller Oremus. An abridgment of the above. Cloth, 9d., with red edges, 1s.; roan or French morocco, 2s.; calf or morocco, 3s.

Path to Paradise. 32 full-page Illustrations. 32mo., cloth, 3d. With 50 Illustrations, cloth, 4d. Superior edition, 6d. and 1s.

Public Devotions, and Serving Boy's Manual. Containing all those Prayers and Devotions for Sundays and Holidays, usually divided in their recitation between the Priest and the Congregation. Compiled from approved sources, and adapted to Churches served either by the Secular or the Regular Clergy, 32mo., Embossed, 1s.; with Epistles and Gospels, 1s. 6d.; French morocco, 2s., with Epistles and Gospels, 2s. 6d.; calf, 4s., with Epistles and Gospels, 4s. 6d.

S. Patrick's Manual. Compiled by Sister Mary Frances Clare. 3s. 6d.

Sure Way to Heaven. Cloth, 6d.: Persian, 2s. 6d.; morocco, 3s. 6d.

Treasury of the Sacred Heart. 18mo., 3s. 6d.; roan, 4s. 6d. 32mo., 2s.; French morocco, 2s. 6d.; calf 5s.; morocco, 6s.

Ursuline Manual. 18mo., 4s.; Persian calf, 7s. 6d.; morocco, 10s.

R. Washbourne, 18 *Paternoster Row, London.*

Garden of the Soul. (WASHBOURNE'S EDITION.) Edited by the Rev. R. G. Davis. *With Imprimatur of the Cardinal Abp. of Westminster.* Twenty-third Thousand. This Edition retains all the Devotions that have made the GARDEN OF THE SOUL, now for many generations, the well-known Prayer-book for English Catholics. During many years various Devotions have been introduced, and, in the form of appendices, have been added to other editions. These have now been incorporated into the body of the work, and, together with the Devotions to the Sacred Heart, to Saint Joseph, to the Guardian Angels, the Itinerarium, and other important additions, render this edition pre-eminently the Manual of Prayer, for both public and private use. The version of the Psalms has been carefully revised, and strictly conformed to the Douay translation of the Bible, published with the approbation of the LATE CARDINAL WISEMAN. The Forms of administering the Sacraments have been carefully translated, *as also the rubrical directions,* from the Ordo Administrandi Sacramenta. To enable all present, either at baptisms or other public administrations of the Sacraments, to pay due attention to the sacred rites, the Forms are inserted without any curtailment, both in Latin and English. The Devotions at Mass have been carefully revised, and enriched by copious adaptations from the prayers of the Missal. The preparation for the Sacraments of Penance and the Holy Eucharist have been the objects of especial care, to adapt them to the wants of those whose religious instruction may be deficient. Great attention has been paid to the quality of the paper and to the size of type used in the printing, to obviate that weariness so distressing to the eyes, caused by the use of books printed in small close type and on inferior paper.

32mo. Embossed, 1s. ; with rims and clasp, 1s. 6d. ; with Epistles and Gospels, 1s. 6d.; with rims and clasp, 2s. French morocco, 2s.; with rims and clasp, 2s. 6d.; with E. and G., 2s. 6d.; with rims and clasp, 3s. French morocco extra gilt, 2s. 6d. ; with rims and clasp, 3s.; with E. and G., 3s.; with rims and clasp, 3s. 6d. Calf, or morocco 4s.; with best gilt clasp, 5s. 6d.; with E. and G., 4s. 6d., with best gilt clasp, 6s. Calf or morocco extra gilt, 5s.; with best gilt clasp, 6s. 6d.; with E. and G., 5s. 6d.; with best gilt clasp, 7s. Velvet, with rims and clasp, 7s. 6d., 10s. 6d., and 13s.; with E. and G., 8s., 11s., and 13s. 6d. Russia, antique, with clasp, 8s. 6d., 10s., 12s. 6d.; with E. and G., 9s. 10s. 6d., 13s., with corners and clasps, 20s.; with E. and G., 20s. 6d. Ivory 14s., 16s., 18s., and 20s., with E. and G., 14s., 16s. 6d., 18s. 6d., and 20s. 6d. Morocco antique, 8s. 6d.; with 2 patent clasps, 12s.; with E. and G., 9s. and 12s. 6d. ; with corners and clasps, 18s.; with E. and G., 18s. 6d. ; morocco, with turn-over edges, 7s. 6d. ; with E. and G., 8s.

The Epistles and Gospels. *Complete,* cloth, 6d.; roan, 1s. 6d.

"This is one of the best editions we have seen of one of the best of all our Prayer Books. It is well printed in clear, large type, on good paper." —*Catholic Opinion.* A very complete arrangement of this which is emphatically the Prayer Book of every Catholic household. It is as cheap as it is good, and we heartily recommend it."—*Universe.* "Two striking features are the admirable order displayed throughout the book, and the insertion of the Indulgences in small type above Indulgenced Prayers In the Devotions for Mass, the editor has, with great discrimination, drawn largely on the Church's Prayers, as given us in the Missal."—*Weekly Register.*

R. Washbourne, 18 *Paternoster Row, London.*